FIVE FOR THE MONEY

by Doris Reidy

D1473074

ISBN: 1518688454
ISBN-13: 978-1518688454

To Josh Langston,
writer, teacher, mentor and friend,
without whose encouragement
this book would never have been written.

CHAPTER ONE

Starshine Greene

"We won! We won! We won!"

I struggled to open my eyes. The voice on my phone kept screaming an incomprehensible message at a pitch best suited for dog whistles.

"Who *is* this?"

Exhausted from a stressful work week, I'd fallen into bed early on Friday night and gone right to sleep. Eleven-thirty seemed like the black middle of nowhere and I couldn't make sense of the wild jabbering in my ear. I held the phone out several inches.

"It's Bella. Star, are you awake? We won, Star! We won the lottery."

"Bella? Calm down; I couldn't even tell it was you. You mean we won a couple hundred bucks like last time? What's all that shouting behind you? Where are you, anyway? Are you calling from a bar?"

"No! Not a couple hundred bucks! Two hundred twenty-five million bucks! I just watched the drawing on the 11 o'clock news and I wrote down the numbers like I always do. Then I went over our five tickets one by one, and Star, the last ticket had all the numbers. We actually won! Can you believe it?"

"No, I can't," I said flatly. "You must be mistaken. Maybe you wrote down the numbers wrong. Let's check the morning newspaper. In the meantime, just put the tickets in a safe place."

"Oh." Bella exhaled a long, disappointed breath. I heard her say, "Hush, Miguel. I can hardly hear Star." And then back to me: "Maybe you're right. I guess I could have made a mistake. Sorry I woke you. Bye."

I settled back under the covers, noting that Rowan had not so much as stirred. Dear little Bella: so young and full of enthusiasm. Still, it wasn't like her to-- My cell phone's ringtone shattered my hope of sleep. I grabbed for it, fumbled it to the floor and then had to get on my hands and knees to fish it out from under the bed.

"Dammit! Bella? Is that you again?"

"Star, we *did* win." She was more coherent this time, but still giddy with excitement. "I looked up the numbers online and triple checked our ticket. Then I had Miguel check it, and I'm telling you, we won!"

"But are you sure it's the big jackpot? Not one of the smaller ones?"

"Yes. Two. Hundred. Twenty-five. Million. Dollars."

She wasn't kidding. It took a minute for the news to sink in. Then I shook Rowan non-too gently by the shoulder.

"Holy crap. Rowan, wake up! We won! We're rich!"

Rowan turned over and opened one bleary eye. "Huh? Won what? Who's on the phone?"

"It's Bella. She's saying our office pool hit the jackpot. You know how every Friday, five of us throw in a dollar and buy lottery tickets? Bella says one of our tickets won. She's triple-checked."

Screaming sounds were coming from the phone. Rowan sat up, suddenly wide-awake.

"Where's that ticket?" he asked.

"Bella!" I yelled into the phone. "Bella, be quiet a minute. Where is the winning ticket?"

"Right here in my hand. I'm looking at it. What should I do, Star? Should I hide it?"

"Um, where's Miguel?"

"He's right here. Should I have him keep it for us?"

"No! I mean, no, you hang onto it. Put it in your billfold and sit on it until we get there. Don't let anybody else touch it. Have you called the others yet?"

"You were the first one I called."

"Okay, wait to call the others until Rowan and I are with you. We'll be there in twenty minutes. Sit on that billfold, Bella, I'm not kidding!"

~*~

It was pure bad luck that a person named Starshine should marry a man named Greene. In fact, I had a moment of serious hesitation before I agreed to marry Rowan Greene for just that reason. My parents had resisted the temptation to make up a name that sounded African when I was born in

1977, but they couldn't quite bring themselves to name me Mary or Jane, either. So, being gentle souls, they waxed poetic, and I got stuck with Starshine which isn't so bad shortened to Star. I also got stuck with lots of touchy-feely character traits that make me a sucker for hard-luck stories, stray animals and suffering of any kind. Okay, I recycle and hug trees and all that, but still: Starshine Greene? It's a little embarrassing.

I work in Centerville city government in what is known as Section Eight Housing, a government agency that puts poor people in heavily subsidized dwellings. There are always too many applicants and not enough places. The waiting list is years long and constantly replenishes itself like a magic porridge pot. My job is to talk to the people who come in crying, demanding, threatening and begging for a place to stay. Most days I have to say, "No, no, we can't help you, your income is too high, you're on probation, you have a felony conviction, or for whatever reason, you don't meet the criteria sent down from on high." It is hard.

Every Friday, I treat myself to a lunch that's not from a brown paper bag with my best work buddy, Bella Morales. Bella works in the mayor's office and while you'd think she'd be a veritable font of workplace gossip, she's as close-mouthed as a sock monkey. If you ever heard anything juicy, you sure didn't hear it from Bella. I like her for that, and for her happy nature and her dream. Bella wants to be a country singer. She just knows she could make it if she could catch a break.

"Chained to the paycheck, that's my trouble,"

she'd say. "How can I go to Nashville and get discovered when I need to pay my rent?"

Bella never complained about the constant financial drain named Miguel, her boyfriend. I found it hard to understand why a girl as young, pretty and talented as Bella let herself be dragged down by a smoldering loser like Miguel. But my folks were big on tolerance. Mom sang the Beatles song, "Let It Be," around the house all the time. So I let Bella be.

After lunch, we'd always stop by the 7-11 closest to the office and buy lottery tickets. There were five of us in a pool and we'd throw in a dollar every Friday morning with the strict understanding that any winnings were to be divided evenly with no further discussion. We even put that in writing and everyone signed it.

The most we ever won was a couple hundred dollars. We deliberately didn't talk about the odds against winning, the comparisons to being struck by lightning or elected president, because there was that little space between buying the tickets and knowing for sure that we didn't win. It was a golden field of dreams where all things were possible and it was well worth a dollar a week.

"What would you do if you won?" was the topic of many lunch conversations. Bella said she'd quit her job the same day and go to Nashville.

"If I could only get someone to listen to me sing," she said wistfully. "If I had money to get a voice coach and cut a demo, I could make it, I really believe I could make it."

My plans for the big jackpot were different. I saw myself as the family Mother Teresa, Fixer of

Everything.

"Rowan and I could travel. We've always wanted to go to Africa and volunteer in a school. Just think of the adventure! And I could help out my sisters and pay off my folks' mortgage. They should have their house paid for before they retire. All our nieces and nephews could go to college and not have student loans."

"But what about *you?*" Bella asked me once. "After you and Rowan get back from educating all those African kids, what then? Don't you want a new car and a fancy house?"

"Well-- I guess-- I've never really thought about it." Yep, Saint Star, that was me. Well, the time to think about it had come.

~*~

Rowan cut the headlights as we pulled into the parking area of Bella's apartment complex. No point in drawing any curious neighbors to peer through their curtains. Bella's third floor windows were wide open and conspicuously ablaze. There was a definite odor of pot wafting down on the breeze.

"That would be Miguel." Rowan whispered.

We climbed the three flights, shoes in hand, feeling like we were on a secret mission. Bella opened the door just as my hand was raised to knock on it.

"We won, we won, we won!" she scream-whispered.

"Where's that billfold, Bella?" I asked.

"I'm holding it, see: it's right here."

"Good. Could we have a look at the ticket?"

"Sure, feast your eyes. And look here, I've got the lottery numbers pulled up on my computer. 36-18-44-70-12, and we even hit the Power Ball, 5. Do you know what that comes to? Do you?"

"Two hundred twenty-five million dollars," I said. My tongue felt thick. "I was doing the math on the way over. That's forty-five million for each of us. Taking the one-time payout, it's less than that, and then taxes have to come off the top but it's still just – just so darn much money!"

Miguel, his eyes as pink as a rabbit's, swung Bella around in a staggering kind of happy dance.

"Shh! Don't wake up all your neighbors. We don't want to attract any attention," I said. "We need to tell the others; should we call them now or wait until morning?"

"Would you have wanted to wait until morning?" Bella asked.

"Gosh, no. Let's call!"

And so we did. We simply couldn't wait to relive that out-of-body moment of realization with our lottery buddies. We called Darren Davis first. His mother answered the phone after twelve rings, and she did not sound happy about being awakened.

"Darren is asleep," she said icily, "and why on earth are you calling him at this hour?"

"Would you please get him, Mrs. Davis?" I said. "It's extremely important."

I heard her martyred sigh, heavy footsteps and a knock on what was presumably Darren's door.

"Darren, wake up. Some lunatic is calling for

you and says it's important."

There was an interval of shuffling feet and throat-clearing.

"They must still have a land-line," I whispered to Bella. "Imagine Mr. Techie not sleeping with his Smartphone."

"His mother probably makes him put it away with his toys before bedtime," Bella whispered back.

It was well known at the office that Darren Davis, a whiz at all things technical, still lived with his mother. His shirts and handkerchiefs were always spotless and flawlessly pressed and you just knew it was not by his hand. Rumor had it his mom put a balanced meal on the table every night at six sharp, and Darren had darn well better be there to eat it. Still, he was a nice guy, just a bit socially awkward. I wondered how having so much money would change his life. For that matter, I wondered how it would change mine.

~*~

The thing is, I care too much for my own good what happens to people, and not only my friends. The strangers who come into my office begging for a home rip my heart out. That very day, a young mom showed up trailing her five children behind her. She was in tears. The kids all had huge scared eyes and they were unnaturally quiet -- hunkered down like little bunnies.

"Please, ma'am, we are desperate," she said. "My husband left me with the kids and no money. We sleep in the shelter at night but there's no place to stay during the day, so we just walk around. Please help us. Please."

And I had to say all I could do was put them on the waiting list. I gave her a photocopied roster of area churches and charities that helped with food and housing until their money ran out, usually by June. She looked at it and cried harder.

"How would I get to these places? There's no bus, and even if there was, I don't have bus fare for all of us."

In the end, I told my co-workers I needed a personal hour away from the office. I loaded the woman, whose name was Jane Kaufman, and her kids into my car, drove to a Motel Six and paid for a room with a kitchenette for a week. Then I took them to the grocery store and bought enough food to feed them for a while. They were so grateful that I was embarrassed. It made me mad that they had to depend on such stop-gap charity as mine. Yes, they had a roof over their heads and the kids could take baths and eat supper -- for a week. Then what would become of this family? It was all I could do and it wasn't nearly enough.

~*~

When Darren finally made it to the phone, he sounded nothing like the timid techie we knew at work. I hit the button for speakerphone.

"What the hell? Who is this, anyway?"

"Darren, it's Star. I'm calling with good news. Are you awake?"

"Yeah, I am now. What is it?"

"Darren, we won the lottery! We won, Darren, two hundred twenty five million dollars."

"Are you drunk? This isn't funny. You woke up my Mom and me with this nonsense?"

"No, really, Darren, I'm not kidding...."

But all we heard was a click and a dial tone. Wide-eyed, I pressed the End Call button on the phone. So much for sharing the joy.

After that debacle, we debated whether to awaken Marilyn with the news. She cares for her elderly mother as well as working full-time, and sleep is a precious commodity. Would Marilyn rather sleep now and rejoice in the morning? Since it was Friday night and none of us had to be at work the next day, we decided to wait. Rested, she'd have the whole weekend to assimilate the news.

Scott Holmes was the last of our five some. He and his wife had two little ones and I'd heard rumors of a third on the way, although he hadn't announced it yet. Scott was okay to work with, but I didn't really like him much. He made mean remarks about Jessie, his wife, for one thing, and complained constantly about the time and money required to raise a family. If another baby was indeed in the offing, then bitterness wasn't working well as birth control.

Scott could have still been up although by now it was going on one AM, but the phone might wake the kids. And I had a gut feeling his wife needed to be present when he heard the news.

"Let's wait until morning to tell Scott, too."

Miguel actually produced a pot of coffee with his own little hands, and the four of us sat around

Bella's living room drinking it. Whenever we caught each other's eyes, big tired grins split our faces. We were all exhausted, but no one felt sleepy. Our minds were spinning with what this unimaginable pile of money would mean in our lives. I knew one thing: I'd find that young mother and her children and they'd have more than a cheap motel room for a week. I could hardly wait.

~*~

"The first thing we have to do is safeguard that ticket," Rowan said. "Star, you and Bella should sign the back of it, with me and Miguel as witnesses. Tomorrow, Darren, Marilyn and Scott should sign."

"Hey, man, what about us, shouldn't we sign it, too?" Miguel asked.

"Did you contribute to the pool to buy it? I didn't. This is a deal between five co-workers and the money belongs to them, not us," Rowan said.

"Of course, we'll share, honey," Bella said quickly.

"That's entirely up to you," Rowan said. "For now let's think of the safest place to keep that ticket until morning, when it should be put in a safety deposit box in a bank."

"You keep it, Star," Bella said. "You and Rowan live in a house, not an apartment, so there aren't as many people around. Do you still have that old safe in your basement?"

"We do. I guess that would be as secure a place as any for the rest of the night. The bank opens at ten; why don't you come over a little before that and we'll go together to get a safety deposit box. Better yet, come about nine and we'll call the others. They might want to go to the bank with us."

"Bella, Miguel, tell no one about this," Rowan said, looking hard at Miguel. "When the news gets out that you five have come into all this money, you're going to be caught up in a firestorm you can't even imagine. From what I've read about lottery winners, the local and national media will come calling immediately, demanding statements and pictures, and you will hear from family and friends and strangers who all need some of your money. It's vital that you are prepared with a plan before that happens. You're going to need financial advisors and lawyers and accountants. It will take some time to get all that organized and during that time, you've got to keep it quiet."

~*~

My eyes were wide open in the dark. Rowan and I went back to bed after returning from Bella's, and Rowan was actually sleeping. Sleep had never seemed farther away for me, although my eyeballs felt like they'd been rolled in sand.

All that money. I could quit my job. Rowan could quit his job. We could go to Africa-- or anywhere. I pictured the delighted faces of my sisters when I paid off their mortgages and bought everyone new cars. My parents. I knew they were going through a tough time financially although they hadn't said a word to any of us. They tried to save every available penny for a decent retirement and it meant a bare-bones budget. This money meant that they could stop worrying, stop working and enjoy life. My oldest nephew, Jimmy, a bright kid, a rising senior in high school with the grades for college but not the money -- now he could go and study whatever he liked. Why, he could be the family's first doctor. With him blazing the trail, all the other kids would probably follow him to higher education and good careers. Our family status could go from blue-collar to white-collar in one generation.

I thought about spending money on myself. I'm not yet forty and people say I look like I'm in my twenties. That might be a stretch; maybe they're just being nice. I've stayed slim, and I wear my hair natural, in a small, tidy Afro. Maybe I'll start using a bit of make-up. Bella says I'm a prime candidate for a make-over. She makes me go shopping with her and tries to get me into the kind of clothes she wears -- the latest fashions. I can't pretend to drum up any interest, even for Bella. The thought of pouring myself into the skintight clothes we see in the shops and cramming my poor feet into four-inch stiletto heels just makes me laugh. Besides, Rowan likes the way I look, and who else do I have to please?

The house, now, that's a different matter. I'm more interested in adorning the house than myself. In the nightlight's gentle glow, I take stock of our bedroom. The four-poster bed was purchased in pieces at a garage sale and we restored it ourselves. The house smelled like varnish for weeks when we refinished the hardwood floors with a rented sander. Grandma's hand-stitched Dresden Plate quilt hangs full length on one wall. In the daylight, it glows with color, and I drew from those colors when I decorated the rest of the room. It's a lovely, peaceful room, I think. Every bit of this little ranch house is beautiful to me because I've put so much of myself into it.

I thought about what the money could do for our home. We could get the driveway resurfaced. Or even have a new one poured. I guess we could get a new house, for that matter, but I don't really want one. And Rowan's old car has just about had it. We could get another -- any kind he likes. We don't have to worry about depreciation, or whether it will hold resale value. We could hire house painters instead of doing it ourselves. We could replace that ratty carpet in the den. Oh, and maybe do some landscaping. I wonder what sod costs. Wait, it doesn't matter what it costs!

Looking back, my dreams were naïve. But they filled my head as my eyes finally closed and I slept the last sleep of my old life. When I woke up, everything was different.

~*~

At first I didn't remember what had happened. In the same way that memory brings bad news crashing back into your mind after a night's sleep, memory brought me the good news -- the great news! -- that Rowan and I were rich today. Yesterday we'd been paycheck people; today was the beginning of our new lives.

We had the pleasant task of telling the other members of the pool, Marilyn and Scott, and making sure that Darren understood what I'd told him on the phone last night. He hadn't sounded very with it. I wondered if he'd been drinking, but then I remembered his ferocious mother. Not much chance of getting away with anything on her watch.

Rowan and I took our coffee cups out on the front porch because there just didn't seem to be enough air in the house. Being rich apparently takes more oxygen. So we were there when Darren pulled up and that's when we told him. I hate it that he threw up in my hydrangea bushes. Now I'll have to get the hose out and wash that disgusting stuff away. Being rich apparently upsets the stomach, too.

CHAPTER TWO

Darren Davis

I can't believe I went right back to sleep after Star's phone call. You'd think I get middle-of-the-night calls telling me I'm a millionaire all the time. To be truthful, I was a little drunk when I answered the phone. Mom was standing right there in her pink chenille robe, breathing fire, and I couldn't think straight. It was easier to pass it off as a prank call and go back to bed.

Mom would kill me if she knew I keep vodka in my room. She is totally against drinking alcohol. Totally. I told her I was reorganizing my closet and put up a couple of shelves. That was to cover up a little hidey-hole I made between the wall studs. I have to be pretty crafty to fool my mom. She cleans every inch of the house and would find my stash any place else, but I outfoxed her this time. I like to have a few drinks after she goes to bed. Well, hell, I'm a grown man.

So maybe if I hadn't had a couple -- more than a couple, it was Friday night, after all -- I would have remembered that Star isn't the kind of person who makes prank calls. But I crawled into my still-warm bed and went back to sleep and when I woke up the next morning her call seemed like a dream.

Mom had a list of errands for me to run. She says she does everything else around the place so the least I can do is run errands, which she hates. That's what I do every Saturday morning. It's a small price to pay, really, for all she does for me: laundry, cooking, cleaning -- she even cuts the grass.

This morning I had a rip-roaring headache and it must have shown because she said, "Darren, are you sick? Do you need to go back to bed, son?"

"No, Mom, I'm fine, just a little headache. It will go away after I eat."

So then, of course, she started cooking and I had to choke down a huge breakfast of sausage and fried eggs and biscuits. It helped the headache but did nothing at all for my queasy stomach.

After a long, tiresome exchange about whether I felt better, whether I felt well enough to run errands, whether I should perhaps take some aspirin and whether I might be coming down with something, I finally escaped. Errands had never seemed so good.

My first stop was Star's place. I thought I'd just run in and apologize for being so grouchy on the phone. I have to work with her; no point in having an issue. I found her and Rowan sitting on the front porch having coffee.

"Morning, Star, Rowan," I said. "I stopped by to say I'm sorry if I sounded grumpy when you called last night. You *did c*all, didn't you?"

"Call?" Star said. "Let's see -- I think I vaguely remember making a phone call. But then again, why would I call just to tell you that we won the lottery?"

"Yeah." I tried to laugh a little, keep it light. She didn't seem like herself and I couldn't tell if she was mad or not. "Why would I want to know that?"

"Darren, you big dummy, we did win! We won the grand prize. You're a millionaire."

"Sure, Star, quit messing around. I've got a bad head today."

"Well, it's going to get a lot better when the news finally penetrates. I'm not kidding. Our little 'ol office pool won two hundred twenty-five million dollars. You put your dollar in the pot yesterday morning. Today you're a millionaire."

Time slowed down. I gradually grasped that Star was serious. I sat down abruptly; I stood up just as abruptly and lost the eggs and sausage in the hydrangea bushes beside the porch. I was laughing but tears were mixing with the slick sweat of nausea on my face. I was a disgusting mess, but I was a *rich* disgusting mess.

What will Mom say?

I decided not to tell her right away. I just wanted to think about it by myself for a day or two. Once I tell Mom something -- anything -- she starts finding solutions. (Witness this morning's breakfast, now residing in the bushes.) Mom could have my share of the money invested at the highest rate of return in about half an hour. And that's allowing time for her to be convinced that we really won. I've always told her everything important in my life, but now... well, I'm going to wait a little while.

~*~

Star and Rowan were talking and gradually I could hear them again.

"Darren, you need to sign the ticket on the back. Bella and I have already signed and we all need to so there won't be a problem about who shares in the pay-out," Star said.

"Come on, let's go downstairs to the safe and I'll get it out just long enough for you to sign," Rowan said.

He stood and led the way to the basement. In single file, we descended the narrow stairs and entered the shadowy underbelly of the house. Star switched on an overhead light that shone like a spotlight on a big, black monolith squatting beside the furnace.

"Where in the world did you get this monstrosity of a safe?" I asked. "And how did you ever get it down here?"

"It was here when we bought the house. The previous owner didn't want to mess with it, so he just eased on out of town and left it right where you see it. He wrote down the combination and taped it to the door; otherwise, we would have had to blow the damn thing up to get it open."

"But were we glad to have it last night," Star said. "I knew once the ticket was in this safe, it wasn't going anywhere."

With some ceremony, Rowan twirled the dial and entered the combination. He turned the handle. Nothing. He twirled and entered again. Still nothing.

"Rowan, what's wrong? Why won't it open?" Star said, her voice rising two octaves.

Marilyn Simmons

"Marilyn... Marilyn... Marilyn...."

I knew the quavering old voice would keep calling my name until hell froze over or I got up, whichever came first. My limbs felt leaden but somehow I managed to fight my way up from a deep cave of sleep and hoist myself upright. Throwing back the covers and leaving my warm bed was almost a physical hurt.

"Coming, Mom," I croaked.

When I shuffled to the threshold of her room, the smell of fresh urine hit me and I knew the reason for her call was that she'd wet the bed again. Second time that night. Offering my arm as a grab bar, I helped her inch herself into a sitting position. I swung her tiny old legs over the edge of the bed and she raised her arms like a child so I could strip off the sodden nightgown.

"I'm sorry, honey," she said. "I don't know what's wrong with me, to keep doing this. It makes so much work for you."

"There are things you can wear, you know, Mom," I said, trying to keep the impatience out of my voice.

"You mean diapers," she said. "I just hate the thought of wearing diapers!"

"Well, we don't have to decide about that tonight," I said, shaking out a clean gown. "Here, put your arms in the sleeves. Tomorrow we'll get you a nice warm bath, but for tonight, let's just get you and the bed dry."

Half an hour later I stuffed the wet sheets and blankets into a basket in the laundry room with the others. Tomorrow's going to be a big laundry day, I thought, returning to bed. But sleep was gone for the night, no matter how tired I felt. In its place came a pack of snarling, snapping, yapping thoughts that would continue to gnaw on me until dawn.

How can I keep this up? I'm sixty-one years old and I'm so tired. What will happen to Mom if I get sick? I have to keep working until I'm sixty-seven before I file for Social Security so I'll get the maximum benefit; what if I can't make it 'til then? What will we do if Mom has to go to a nursing home? We don't have that kind of money. It would take every penny she has and all that I've managed to save for retirement and it still wouldn't be enough. Then what would I live on after she's gone and I'm too old to work?

Finally, I gave up on sleep, got up and tiptoed to the kitchen to make coffee. Mom's hearing was keen despite her age, and I didn't want her company just now. Thankful that our 1960's-era house was too old to be "open concept" and still had defined rooms, I quietly closed the kitchen door before I turned on the light.

My library book was open on the kitchen table where I'd left it when I went to bed. I sat down with my coffee cup, rubbed my gritty eyes and began to read where I'd left off. At least I had that -- the world of books, the world that books brought to me. My escape. Eventually, my head drooped and the book became a pillow. I didn't hear the first birdsong of dawn.

~*~

Mom woke again at eight, and I got her bathed, into clean clothes and established in her recliner to have her breakfast on a tray before I began the laundry. The old washer would get a workout today, but the sun was shining and I would be able to hang the bedding out to dry. That saved a few cents in electricity and Mom loved the smell of sheets dried in the fresh air.

I wasn't at all prepared to hear a knock on the door. It was close to noon and I'd been hard at work for hours. I wore my oldest around-the-house clothes and had brushed my teeth and my hair, but that was as far as I'd gotten; I was certainly not ready for company. Yet there stood Bella, Star and Darren from the office. I couldn't hide my surprise.

"Well, my goodness, what brings you all here on a Saturday? Did the office burn down?"

"Nothing's wrong, Marilyn. May we come in?" Star said.

All three of them had an air of barely suppressed excitement. I couldn't imagine what it was all about.

"Yes, of course, come in," I said. "It's some of my co-workers, Mom, just dropped by for coffee."

"Bring them in here, honey," she called back. She loves company and gets almost none.

"Okay, just give us a few minutes and they'll come in and say hello." I raised my eyebrows questioningly and they all nodded. They're nice people and, whatever crisis brought them to my door, they remembered their manners.

Nothing could have prepared me for the

news they gave me that morning. At first it all ran together in my head. Lottery, millions, -- I couldn't make sense of what they were saying. Star took my hands in both of hers and got right in my face.

"Marilyn. Listen. Our lottery pool won the big prize last night. We will each get millions of dollars. We aren't sure exactly how much it will be after taxes, but we think around $18 million apiece. Do you understand what I'm saying?"

She produced the ticket and showed me where to sign and date it on the back. I took the pen she offered in my shaking hand and wrote my name. Then it finally sank in, and I sank, too, right down to the floor. They gathered around and lifted me up by the elbows, all laughing and talking at once.

Mom kept calling for us to join her in the front room. "What's going on out there? It sounds like a big party, all that laughing and talking. Come tell me about it."

So we all trooped in and told my mother the news that meant whatever worries she had about being a financial burden were over, and that from now on her old age would be a time of peace and comfort. I'm not sure she took it in. Or maybe at that age nothing can surprise a person. She just nodded and said, "Well, isn't that nice! Isn't that nice for you, honey!"

Scott Holmes

"Scott, the baby's crying. It's your turn. Scott!"

"Chrissake, Jessie, I've got to get up in the morning!"

"I've been up three times with him. C'mon, it's your turn."

I threw back the covers violently, making sure to uncover Jessie from her warm little nest at my side. *Serves her right. The kids are her job. I'm the one who's got to work tomorrow to support this zoo.* I padded barefoot into Daniel's room, where the little tyrant stood screaming, shaking the bars of his crib.

"Okay, okay, Danny, simmer down," I said, lifting my 8-month old son into my arms. The screams immediately subsided into hiccups and sniffles. Daniel wanted his father to know that he'd suffered.

After I did some back-rubbing and shuffling around the room, Daniel's head began to droop onto my shoulder. The clock said 5:35 AM when he finally gave up his fight to stay awake and I was able to tuck him back into his crib. By then I was wide awake myself and knew that if I returned to bed and slept an hour or so until the alarm went off at 7:00, I'd feel like crap all day, and if I didn't sleep any more -- *yeah, I'll feel like crap all day.*

I went downstairs to the living room, turned the television on low and curled up under an inadequate crocheted afghan. *I'm not going to sleep* was my last conscious thought.

I was flying; the road beneath my wheels felt like silk as the powerful car devoured the miles. The sun warmed my back and the wind blew my hair, which was suddenly abundant. I had no responsibilities, no chores, and no job. I felt a surge of happiness and well-being. Beside the road I saw Jessie and the kids, waving their arms, crying stop, stop and take us along. *But I didn't stop, I didn't even wave. They were out of sight in a second. But then there they were, right in the car with me. I remember thinking that I must be dreaming. Daniel was screaming, Katie's nose was running disgustingly, and Jessie sat with her legs apart to accommodate her stomach, distended with the next little Holmes. I pushed the gas pedal to the floor, but the car was slowing, slowing, the powerful engine sputtering. We rolled to a stop....*

I jerked awake tangled in the afghan, feeling cold sweat under my arms and a miserable headache forming behind my eyes. The television quietly told itself the morning news and elsewhere in the house I heard a toilet flush. The day had begun. The only bright spot on the horizon was that it was Friday.

~*~

Saturday morning was one of those bright, clear days that inspire some people to take to the open road and other people to paint the house. I'm one of the open road people; Jessie's a painter. The list of chores she could dream up just over breakfast was staggering. I looked at her and made sure she saw my disgust and dislike.

"And then I thought we could take the kids shopping for new shoes, and... Scott, why are you looking at me like that?"

"Because you're a taskmaster; all you do is crack the whip across my back. I'm sick of it, Jessie."

"But -- don't be mad, Scotty. Never mind all the stuff I just said, we don't have to do it."

Jessie's eyes filled with tears. In early pregnancy she was always a crybaby, and I hated to be cried at. It aroused no sympathy in me, none at all. In fact, it pissed me off.

The doorbell rang and I jumped up to answer it. Anything was better than sitting there watching Jessie try not to cry. I was astonished to see Star and Bella, two of my co-workers, standing on the porch.

"Good morning, Scott," Star said. She seemed to be crackling with excitement. Bella's dark eyes sparkled and she bounced a little on her toes.

"Uh, well, good morning. What are you doing here? I mean, what brings you here on a Saturday?" I tried to inject a hint of warmth into my voice.

"We need to talk to you and Jessie, if you've got a minute," Star said.

"Well, I guess... sure, come on in. Jessie," I called, "we've got company."

Jessie hurried to the door. She knew Bella and Star the way you know people who work with your spouse, but you'd have thought they were her long-lost friends and that unexpected callers at 9 o'clock on a Saturday morning were just what she was hoping for.

"Come in, come in! Bella, Star, what a nice surprise. How about a cup of coffee? Here, let me clear off this chair, Katie left her crayons all over the place. Sit, sit, please. Can I get you anything?"

Bella and Star settled at our messy kitchen table, coffee cups in hand. I looked at them with raised eyebrows, waiting for an explanation of this unprecedented visit. Bella spoke first.

"Scott, you know how our little pool always

buys a lottery ticket on Friday?"

"Yeah, I know. I put in my dollar yesterday, didn't I?" I was reaching for my billfold, figuring I'd forgotten my contribution.

"You did, Scott, you put in your dollar. We're here to tell you," Bella stopped speaking and exchanged a giddy look with Star. "We're here to tell you that we won! We won the big lottery prize last night, Scott. We're rich, all of us."

I just stared at her. Beside me, I heard Jessie emit a tiny squeak, sounding very much like a mouse. A pregnant little mouse.

"How much?" I managed to get out of my dry mouth.

"We don't know for sure, but our rough estimate is about $18 million apiece, after taxes."

Of course there were incredulous questions -- mine -- and screaming and crying from Jessie and hugs and reassurances from Star and Bella. The kids picked up on the excitement and reacted by raising the decibel level even higher. The chore list and shoe-shopping trip were completely forgotten. I remembered my dream. Maybe that car would pick up some speed now and drive me to a new life.

CHAPTER THREE

Star

Rowan finally did get that old safe open again, after a few sweaty moments in which he took some deep, calming breaths and worked the combination very slowly and carefully. By noon of that first day, everyone had signed the back of the lottery ticket and we'd gone to the bank and purchased a safety deposit box for it. We gathered that night in my kitchen to discuss what to do next.

Scott was in favor of claiming the money right away. "The sooner it's in my bank account, the better," he kept saying.

Marilyn wanted some time to get used to the idea. She seemed reluctant to think, let alone talk, about how the money would change her life. Her daily routine may be the hardest of any of us, and yet she seemed strangely reluctant to change it.

Bella could only think down the road to Nashville.

"Bella, we have some ground to cover at home, first," Rowan said.

He was always the pragmatic one, proceeding step by cautious step. Miguel didn't say much but he never left Bella's side and watched her with his inscrutable black eyes like a cat watches a canary.

Darren was anxious about telling his mother that he'd won and he also wanted more time to assimilate the news himself.

"Mom will try to manage it for me," he said, "but I want to have a game plan before I even tell her."

Rowan and I just kept looking at each other and breaking into big grins. I was so grateful for his calm and measured advice. I'd never loved him more.

I think the first thing you all should do is talk to a lawyer," he said.

"Already have," Scott said. "I've hired Bickler, Standers and Fraine to represent my interests."

"Wow, that was fast work," Rowan said. "That's one of the biggest law firms in town. Do you suppose they'd be open to representing the rest of the group?"

"You can ask," Scott said, with a shrug.

"I think you'll also need tax accountants and financial advisors," Rowan went on. "It may be that the lottery officials have people they recommend, or Bickler, Standers and Fraine may have staff to handle that for you, too.

The point is, you each need to have a financial plan firmly in place before the world gets wind of your good fortune. You will be hearing from every shirttail relative and distant acquaintance you've ever had the minute the news becomes public. To be able to say that your money is invested, or that you're in the process of forming a foundation

-- or whatever, will be much easier than having to say no to all the requests for money that will pour in."

"I notice you keep saying 'you,'" Miguel said. "Are you not sharing in Star's winnings?"

"That's for Star to decide," said Rowan, glaring at Miguel, who smiled and turned away. Bella will have trouble with that one.

Together, we decided to take the following week to consult with lawyers and other experts, agreeing to meet again next Saturday to set a time to claim the money. In the meantime, we promised to tell no one. I hate keeping a secret.

~*~

The first question I had to settle was whether to go to work on Monday. Characteristically, Rowan left it totally up to me.

"I'm going to keep working," he said, "because I didn't win the lottery. You should do what makes you most comfortable."

For my entire adult life, I'd gotten up every weekday morning and gone to work. That might be the exact definition of a rut, but I found great solace in routine. I decided to stick with what I knew, and so I showed up at the office as usual and tried to act like it was just an ordinary day.

When I had a spare moment, I pulled up the file of the woman who had touched me so deeply that I'd gone outside the rules and gotten her and her family a motel room. Her name was Jane Kaufman, and she was now officially languishing on the endless waiting list for housing. I remembered that she and her five kids had one more day in the Motel 6 and when my lunch hour came, I headed there. Pulling into the bleak concrete parking lot, I glanced at the brick façade, broken by even rows of metal-encased windows. Add a few bars and it could be a minimum-security prison. Not the place you'd want to raise children. I was struck once again by the fact that this place was still infinitely preferable to what Jane and the kids had.

She opened the door tentatively to my knock, chain still on, until she recognized me. Then the door and her smile both opened wide.

"Come in, come in" she said, as graciously as if she was inviting me into her own home.

I noted in a sweeping glance that the one room was as neat as it could be, considering six humans were living in it. The children's few possessions were stacked in tidy piles against the wall, the two double beds were made and through the open bathroom door, the towels were neatly hung on the racks. The youngest children, in clean clothes, were eating sandwiches, eyes glued to Sesame Street. Their older siblings, I presumed, were in school.

"Good morning," I said. "I think you remember me? I'm Star Greene, from Section Eight Housing."

"Yes, yes," she said eagerly. "Do you have good news for me, Mrs. Greene? Is there a place for me and my kids to live?"

"Not exactly," I said, watching the light leave her eyes. "Not through Section Eight, anyway. I want to help you and I *can* help -- but as an individual, not as a government employee."

"I don't understand."

"I have had some good luck -- I don't want to say more than that right now -- and I want to share some of it with you."

"But why? Whatever your good luck is, why would you share it with me? I am a stranger to you. You know nothing about me. I can do nothing for you in return."

"I don't want anything in return. And I do know a little something about you. I know you are taking care of five children the best you can under very difficult circumstances. I know you need help, and I can give it."

Jane Kaufman looked at me warily. I couldn't blame her. I was making a hash of this errand of mercy. I should have thought about it more, done some advance planning. Nothing to do now, though, but plow ahead, and so I did.

"Jane, in my job I have to tell so many desperate people that the government can't help them. I always hate it. Something about you and your kids made me hate it even more than usual. Never before have I had the chance to follow up, to make things right -- or at least better. I guess I'm really doing this for myself."

Jane looked increasingly doubtful. I felt like an idiot, babbling about my mysterious good fortune to this leery-eyed woman. I had to laugh at myself.

"Wow, I suck at this, don't I! What I'm trying to say is, I'm going to buy a house as an investment. I thought you might be interested in living in it, kind of be a care-taker for me -- you know, keep up the yard, things like that. When you get a job, you can decide if you want to stay and pay rent, or move on. No obligation."

She frowned. "Why would you need a care-taker? You'd just rent the house out to a tenant," she said logically.

"Well, I don't know anything about being a landlord yet. I thought I might be able to practice on you," I said, with what I hoped was a convincing smile. I sounded lame even to myself. "You'd be doing me a favor, really."

Jane thought for a long moment, emotions playing across her face: skepticism, hope, caution, hope again.

"But why? Why would you do this for me? It's too good to be true; people don't do things like this for total strangers. What's the catch?"

"No catch, truly. I-- well, I came into a lot of money very suddenly. I want to share it, do some good with it. Didn't you ever wish you could just swoop in and help somebody who needs it? I think you and the kids need it right now."

"We do, that's for sure. If you mean it... it doesn't make a lot of sense, but if you really mean it... we would be so grateful. But it would have to be on a business-like basis," she said.

"Oh, of course. Naturally. I wouldn't have it any other way," I said, aware that I was babbling in my relief. "I'll have my lawyer draw up a contract spelling out exactly what each of us agrees to and we'll both sign it."

"And me and the kids could leave any time? It

wouldn't be that we'd owe you money for back-rent or anything if we wanted to leave?"

"Absolutely not. I usually don't trust people who say 'trust me,' but please trust me, Jane. Take this chance. What have you got to lose?"

"I'll have to do something for you in return. Clean your house, watch your children... something to repay you."

"No children, and it's just my husband and me, so our house doesn't need much cleaning, but thank you, Jane. The most important thing would be for you to get a job and make good day-care arrangements for the kids. Then you can start paying your own way. I think you're a person who wants to pay her own way."

"I am. Once we have a home, I know I can get a job. I'm a licensed practical nurse so I have skills to sell, but you can't get a job without a permanent address. Nobody wants an employee who lives in a shelter. I just haven't been able to do anything but survive day-to-day since I've been on my own with the kids."

"Maybe I can help you in your job search, too. I know someone in the Personnel Department at the hospital. I can call her and see what kinds of openings are available."

Jane's face lit up with hope.

"A job!" she said. "If I could only work, I could get us back on our feet. A job would be the *best.*"

We shook hands solemnly, sealing the deal. If I had subconsciously expected a flood of tears, a warm hug and expressions of undying gratitude, I got instead a dignified acceptance of my offers. *This is a woman with self-respect.* And somehow knowing that made it even better.

I promised Jane I would start the house hunt immediately and would be in touch. Then I went by the motel office and paid for another week in advance. While I was at it, I got the adjoining room, too, so there would be more beds for the kids. What the heck. I had the money.

It was a moment of the sweetest sort of satisfaction for me. Life is merciful in unfolding one day at a time. If we knew all that was ahead, would we ever experience joy?

~*~

Rowan and I had our sit-down with Larry Bickler, and he proved to be a goldmine of valuable information. He seemed delighted to have us as clients, but we also connected with him personally. It was reassuring to think we had a friend on our side as we navigated the big-money maze. Larry hooked us up with accountants and financial advisors available through his law firm to give immediate attention to their important and well-heeled clients: us! That was a new feeling. We diversified dutifully, gave gleefully to charity and still had so much left it made our heads hurt.

I'd pay off the mortgages on my sisters' homes, get my brothers-in-law new cars, deposit college funds for each of my nephews and nieces. A monumental moment for me would be presenting my parents with a cashier's check for one million dollars. I envisioned their faces, their surprise and delight and relief.

You know that old saying: money doesn't buy happiness? Well, sometimes it does. This time it would.

Chapter Four

Scott

Later, after I'd gone to Star's house, signed the back of the winning ticket, and we'd all trouped to the bank and deposited it in a safety deposit box, Jessie and I at last had time to talk. She was radiant with happiness.

"We don't have to worry about how we're going to support the new baby," she said, "or putting them all through college when the time comes. Just think, we can remodel, or even move to a bigger place. Katie's been wanting to go to tumbling class, but it was just too expensive, but now...."

"Yeah. Well, we'll see," I said. Her modest ideas of how to manage *my* fortune were depressing me. "I'm thinking the first thing I'll do is replace my car. There's 250,000 miles on that old beater, and it's just a matter of time until it leaves me beside the road somewhere."

"Well, sure, Scotty. You deserve a new car and just think, you'll be able to write a check -- no car payments."

At that moment, the air was pierced with shrieks. Daniel was awake from his nap. Jessie waddled from the room, calling out, "Mama's coming, Danny. Hang on!"

Why does she have to waddle already? She's only about four months pregnant. Geez, the woman has been pregnant more than not since we got married. I remember what she looked like when we met: slim as a reed, but curvy in all the right places. Nobody could wear clothes better than Jessie and nobody looked better without them. Now it's maternity tops and pants with stretchy panels in the front. You'd think a woman as fertile as she is would learn to be more careful with birth control. You'd think she'd care more what she looks like, and want to please her husband. It's all about the kids these days.

Left alone, my mind drifted back to the dream I'd had. The memory of the speeding car, the freedom, the smooth power was made vivid by the knowledge that I could live that dream now. If only I wasn't saddled with Jessie and the kids. But now I could afford a divorce. It wouldn't even be a problem to share some of the money with Jessie. After all, I'm not a monster. I want to look after my family. I just don't want to live with them.

Jessie took advantage of the kids' fascination with a television cartoon to stretch out on the sofa for a few minutes. She was still talking; it felt like she never stopped to draw breath.

"Just think, Scott, we don't have to worry about money anymore."

If she'd said that once, she'd said it a

thousand times. I grunted noncommittally.

"We can take the kids to Disney World, and get a new car big enough for all the car seats when the new baby comes, and get the house painted. Shoot, honey, we can go house-hunting. And if Danny needs corrective shoes... where are you going?"

"I've got a few errands to run," I said on my way out the door. Her litany of petty purchases was too aggravating to listen to any longer. I got in my crappy old car and left.

First stop: the Jaguar dealership on the edge of town. The salesmen didn't come running when they saw me pull up in my old heap. In fact, they barely glanced around from their little conversational huddle when I walked in. I finally had to approach them.

"Could I take a look at some cars, maybe take a test drive?" I asked.

"Look all you want, buddy," one of them said in a smart-alecky voice. "But we only allow test drives for serious buyers."

My Dad used to talk to me in exactly the same tone of voice. The tone that says, "You're a stupid schmuck; you aren't good enough; you aren't much of a son for a man like me." Those memories still echo in my ears.

"Scott! Get the lead out of your ass! Hustle, hustle, hustle!"

"You dumb little prick. I said get me a *Phillips*-head screwdriver."

"No, you can't have a dog. We'd have to tie a pork chop around your neck to get a dog to play with you."

"Eat up, fat boy. Girls like all that lard."

I could hear it all again as if my Dad was right beside me. Some memories never fade, no matter how much you wish they would.

Without another word, I turned and walked out. I heard them laughing as I got back in my car. Well, so much for buying a new Jag. I wouldn't give them the satisfaction after that. But there were plenty of other great cars in the world, and I meant to have one of them just as soon as I got hold of that cash.

I kept driving. I do some of my best thinking when I'm behind the wheel and I had some big thinking to do. The only thing that had been keeping me in my marriage was a lack of funds to get out of it. Now that little problem was solved. People wouldn't take kindly to me leaving a pregnant wife with two small kids, but then, since when did I care what other people thought? I learned early in life to do whatever was necessary to get what I wanted because sure as hell nobody was going to hand it to me. So if it meant beating up a couple of kids to get schoolyard respect, okay. If it meant stealing money out of my old man's billfold while he was sleeping, I did it. If it meant taking my crabby old neighbor's cat and hiding it in our tool shed until it was almost dead, well, that shut the old bag up about my loud music, didn't it? She was too busy calling kitty, kitty, kitty up and down the neighborhood to worry about me. Whatever it takes, just take it. That's always been my motto.

When I met Jessie, it seemed like my luck had

finally changed. She was so sweet and she loved me just the way I was. For a while, I didn't feel like I had to do whatever it took; it felt like I was enough. But then the kids started coming and Jessie got preoccupied with them and forgot about me. So screw it; I'll move on. I've got money now -- I've got a lot of whatever it takes.

The tricky part will be keeping as much of it as possible, although I won't begrudge her enough to take care of the kids. There's plenty to go around. But I don't intend to finance an extravagant lifestyle for them. Disney World, my ass.

I thought I should consult a lawyer. The only ones I knew were the legal counsel the city government used and I didn't think they'd welcome me. Finally, I just walked into the first law office I saw that was open on Saturday, and asked to see whoever was free. That turned out to be a very young man named Lawrence Bickler.

Even the solemn rosewood paneling, deep Oriental carpets and floor-to-ceiling shelves filled with leather-bound law books couldn't lend any gravitas to young Mr. Bickler. He was a slight but wiry little dude, with brown tortoise-shell glasses and a bow-tie he obviously knew how to hand-tie. He looked about sixteen.

"How old are you, anyway?" I asked him.

"I graduated from law school two years ago," he said, "and I've been with Bickler, Standers and Fraine since then."

Okay, a partner's son. Well, what the hell. I explained why I was there.

"So I figured with all that money coming in, I

should have some advice on how to manage it, maybe get an accountant or money manager or something, in addition to a lawyer."

Lawrence's eyes widened. "You are positive that you've won this money?" he asked. "There won't be any controversy about who shares in the pay-out? Sometimes we see a lot of fighting about who was actually in a winning pool."

I'm sure he sees that a lot, I thought scornfully.

"I just signed the winning ticket, which has now been deposited in a bank lock-box. The other winners and I work together and bought tickets as a group every Friday. Here, take a look at this." I handed him my phone with close up photos of the front of the ticket and the signatures on the back. "I don't anticipate any problems with ownership of the jackpot."

"When will you claim the prize?" Lawrence asked.

"According to the rules, we've got thirty days to come forward. I want to have all my ducks in a row before we do."

"Very wise. Well, Mr. Holmes, Bickler, Standers and Fraine will be happy to represent you in this matter. I think we can waive the usual retainer since the funds have not yet come into your possession. Now, I'd like you to meet my father."

Believe me, Mr. Bickler, Senior, was a lot more cordial than those Jag salesmen had been. I left the office feeling like somebody. That's what money can do. I must have looked different, too, because I caught several interested looks from the ladies as I walked back down the street. I decided the next time I talked to Lawrence Bickler, I'd ask him to represent me in divorce proceedings.

Lawrence Bickler

Larry recognized him the minute he walked in -- Scotty Holmes, asshole extraordinaire -- and watched closely to see if Scott remembered him. There was no sign of recognition. He remembered witnessing several of Scott's schoolyard beatings, administered in a workmanlike fashion to smaller kids. Larry had taken great care to stay out of Scott's way, even if it meant going home the long way every day.

As they faced each other, grown men instead of school boys, Larry maintained a neutral expression but permitted himself an inward grin. *Even footing now, huh, jerkface? You're on my turf today.*

Always in the back of Larry's mind was the knowledge that his father was looking anxiously for signs of his incompetence. The youngest of the Bickler children and the only one to follow his father into the legal profession, Larry was still considered the baby by his parents. His law school honors seemed to be regarded on the same level as the nice drawings he brought home from kindergarten. Sweet and all that, but how could little Larry possibly know enough to be a lawyer, let alone a grown-up? He took his promised place in his father's law firm when he passed the bar and began the long process of proving himself. He drew the line, however, at living at home with his parents. A man needed some privacy to live his own life, even if that man's mother still made his dental appointments.

As a very junior staff member, Larry found himself mopping up the mundane tasks that nobody else wanted to do. He understood the importance of paying his dues, especially since nepotism was often implied by his contemporaries, but he was getting increasingly anxious to take on more meaningful work. And now, as luck would have it, Scott Holmes had fallen into his lap, along with his millions of dollars.

Scott's lottery win was irony at its finest: a cruel, callous, undeserving shit hits the jackpot. Larry had heard there were a nice wife and a couple of cute little kids at home, so that made Scott doubly lucky and totally undeserving. But all that aside, Scott was a potentially lucrative client, Larry happened to be the one who caught him when he walked in and he intended to keep him.

Marilyn

Good news can be as upsetting as bad news. That's something I learned from my experience as a lottery winner. Before we won, my life was settled. I knew what to expect, what to hope for, what to worry about. But now everything was upside down. I was supposed to be happy and full of plans but I literally couldn't think what to do next. There was no use trying to talk to Mom about it; she'd just nod and smile. I wanted to shake her and scream, "Mom! What should I do? How should I handle this? What will our lives be like now?" But there was no point in tormenting the poor old soul. She coped with stress by ignoring it.

So I kept on working because that at least gave my days some structure and stability. My co-workers weren't sure how to treat me. Some acted as if my win never happened. Some were extra sweet to me. One of them, Betty, actually came right out and asked me for money. I never liked Betty and she didn't like me, either. We'd always avoided each other as much as possible. But there she was, at my desk one day, asking me to go out for a drink after work.

"Uh, thanks, but I've got to get home to my Mom. She'll be expecting me."

"I could come to your house," Betty said, bold as brass.

"To my house?" I couldn't hide my surprise. "Why?"

"Well, I didn't want to go into it here in the office." Betty looked right and left like a spy in a bad movie. "I have an opportunity for you. I've got a plan to open my own nail salon and get out of this crappy job, be my own boss, you know? But I've just never had the capital to do it. This could be a real deal for you, Marilyn, to make a great return on your investment."

I gazed in horrible fascination at her talon-like nails, painted with green glitter and appliqués, as she drummed them on my desk. Nail salon for witches, I thought. The cackle of the Wicked Witch of the West rang in my head. I can do that cackle to a fare-thee-well and had a strong urge to break it out now. But I controlled myself and forced my eyes up to meet Betty's.

"How kind of you to think of me," I said formally, mental wheels turning fast. "Of course I must consult with my financial advisor. He's strict about my investments. In fact, my money may be all tied up. I'll have to let you know."

Betty glared at me. Clearly, she wasn't counting on charm to win me over. "Fine!" she said. "You do that."

I remembered what Rowan had said about the necessity for professional guidance to deal with the money. The other winners had mentioned an attorney, Lawrence Bickler, and I resolved to go to see him and make sure my words were true: my money *did* need to be all tied up. City workers didn't make big salaries and I'd have loved to help some of them. I wished I had the wisdom of Solomon to be able to sift the deserving from the undeserving. But there were a lot of Bettys out there.

Darren

I don't know how I got stuck so firmly in my mother's web. My college classmates escaped from home as quickly as possible -- graduation and out. In low moments, I suspected it was laziness: I lived rent-free, meals were placed before me and spotless clothing appeared in my closet and dresser drawers as if by magic. It was an easy life and if I sometimes felt like a pampered pet chained to his doghouse -- well, nothing is free in this world, not even magic.

As an only child, I assumed responsibility for

keeping Mom company after Dad died. Her friends took every opportunity to tell me how much it meant to her to have me at home, how lost and lonely she would be if I ever left, and what a dear, good boy I was. So: guilt plus laziness. I just let inertia take over.

Of course, all that comfortable inertia came with a price tag. Mom still treated me like a little boy and worse, I reverted to one when I was with her. My few dating experiences had not been happy ones. Mom didn't like the girls I brought home and she made her unhappiness oppressively apparent. It would have taken a stout-hearted and determined girl to run that one-woman gauntlet of disapproval. Sadly, few were interested enough in me to brave it.

There was one who almost managed, though. Annie. We were high school sweethearts, crazy for each other. I can still close my eyes and see her: small, red-headed, her chin set in determination. We were in the same senior literature class, but I didn't particularly notice her until she presented a paper on why the Tarzan books of Edgar Rice Burroughs counted as literature. The teacher gave her a hard time about it, but she stuck to her guns, citing authors such as Gore Vidal who credited Burroughs' influence in the development of his work. A girl who liked Tarzan! I'd never encountered one before. I was a huge Tarzan fan. The Ape Man had been my hero when I was a scrawny grade-school kid who'd just lost his father.

Immediately after class, I approached her and said that I, too, had read all twenty-three Tarzan books and would she like to go for coffee? She would, we did, and a romance was born, with the instant intensity of teenage love. We took it seriously.

Annie tried to win Mom over at first, talking to her about gardening and television shows and how to get stains out of laundry. When she got back disapproving stares and monosyllables, she went to work on me when we were alone.

Annie would say, "Stand up for me, Darren! You aren't a little boy any longer. Be a man."

Then Mom would tackle me: "Why are you wasting your time on a girl who'll never be suitable? You're neglecting your studies; you had a C on your last report card. A C! Your father would be so disappointed."

Annie again: "Fight for me, Darren. Don't you love me enough to fight for me?"

Mom: "After all I've done for you. All I've sacrificed to give you the chances I never had. To throw it all away on a little brainless girl...."

I tried fruitlessly to make peace between the two women in my life. At first, I argued with Mom and reassured Annie. Then I bargained with Mom and placated Annie. Finally, I lied to both of them, saying whatever would give me a moment's peace. In the end, ears ringing, I caved. I can still see Annie's tear-streaked face when I said we'd have to cool it. We both knew there was no cooling it; Annie was either all in or all out.

"What about us, Darren?" she demanded. "What about our plans to go to the same college and study forestry and then get ranger jobs in a national park or tending a lighthouse together? What about our future dog named Tarzan? What about Darren and Annie, Junior? What about the damn senior prom, for that matter? Is that off, too?"

I hung my head and mumbled that it would probably be better if she made other plans. She took my chin in her hand and turned my face so she could look me squarely in the eyes. "I won't beg," she said, and walked out of my life.

That break-up hurt for years. I told myself it was just kid-stuff and probably wouldn't have worked out anyway. We were so young. But there was never anyone else like Annie.

Now it was easier to go bowling with the guys once a week and forget the whole dating business. I was 34. I wondered if I'd still be living with Mom at 44 and 54. And then what?

~*~

The night before we were all going to the lottery office to claim our prize, I finally had to tell her. By then, I'd talked to the lawyer, the tax accountant and wealth manager. I couldn't stall any longer. There were items about the "mystery winners" every night on the six o'clock news, which we always watched while eating dinner. Mom would make some comment about how money doesn't buy happiness, or how lottery money was ill-gotten gains that profited no one. I'd just grunt. Grunts are a great way to communicate with Mom because she doesn't listen anyway, and all it takes to satisfy her is some sort of non-verbal acquiescence.

After supper, we did the supper dishes. She

preferred to wash everything by hand, convinced that a dishwasher didn't do the job as well as she did. I dried. I'd found, over the years, that it was a good time to talk. In her familiar kitchen -- her kingdom -- wearing yellow rubber gloves and up to her elbows in soap-suds, Mom was always in a good mood.

"Mom," I said, "there's something I need to talk to you about."

"You've got a girl in trouble," she said immediately, her bifocals reflecting the harsh overhead light as she turned to glare at me.

Apparently that was the first thing that sprang to her mind, although I don't know where this mythical girl and I could have done anything troublesome, with me living right under Mom's nose.

"No, Mom, it's actually good news. I don't know if I ever mentioned that I'm in a lottery pool at work."

"You most certainly did *not* mention it," Mom said. "You know how I feel about gambling of any kind, Darren Davis. Your father was a gambling man, and when he died he left me with his debts. You know that. How could you waste your hard-earned money on the lottery?"

She seemed to be working up a good head of steam, so I hastily cut in.

"Now, listen, Mom, here's the thing: we won. We won $225 million, split between the five of us. My share is about $18 million after taxes. We're going to claim it tomorrow."

Silence. Mom's face turned pale and then red. She opened and closed her mouth a couple of times.

I'd never seen my mother at a loss for words before in the entirety of my life. I felt sorry for her.

"Darren. You won? You won all that money? You're going to get all that money?"

"Yes, Mom."

"But do you have to take it? It will spoil everything."

CHAPTER FIVE

Bella

Taking the ticket to the lottery office was as much fun as I've ever had in my life. We all went: Star and Rowan, Marilyn, Darren, Scott, me and Miguel. I noticed Scott didn't bring Jessie; I guess she was home with the kids. Certainly Miguel wasn't going to miss out. He insisted on going along.

Since we worked at the same place, we all had to ask for the morning off. We didn't want to reveal the real reason, so there was a rash of sudden doctor and dentist appointments. Slipping out of the office as inconspicuously as possible, we met in the parking lot, where we all piled into Star's van. It was almost silent in the car as we rode. We all were too busy inside our own heads to have time for conversation.

When we walked into the lottery office, everybody was smiling. There were news cameras and balloons and flowers and a great, big check with our names on it. We all lined up behind the bank of microphones and posed for photographs, and then we "took questions" just like big shots.

Here's something odd -- usually I would have felt tongue-tied as the center of all that curiosity and attention, especially in such a foreign setting. It was ironic that I, who wanted so much to be a performer, was shy about the spotlight. In an office environment where I knew my value, I felt competent and in control. As a performer, I felt like what I was: a little Chicana, daughter of illegal immigrants, with no right to stand up and sing. So I'd forced myself to perform-- in small bars for tips, at the occasional community fund-raiser for one good cause or another, once at a friend's wedding reception -- but it didn't come easily to me. Audiences were always kind and sometimes downright enthusiastic (mostly the bar crowd), but I'd never gotten paid for singing so I didn't think I could call myself a singer. Not a real one.

But money must be the great equalizer because now that I had it, I felt just as confident as anybody in the world. I think the others would say the same, because we were all loose and at ease during the press conference, laughing and cracking jokes with the reporters. When asked what I'd do with my new wealth, I even had the nerve to say I was going to try to make it as a country singer. I'd never come right out and declared that in public before, but I figured I might as well take advantage of the free publicity while I could.

Back at the office, the whole place erupted in cheers. You can't keep $225 million a secret very long. We were everyone's best friends, but I thought I could tell the difference between those who were genuinely glad for us and those who had a speculative gleam in their eyes.

Miguel had tagged along and was basking in

the reflected glow of my good fortune. It was the first time he'd ever visited my office and I intercepted some curious glances among my co-workers. True, we didn't look like a matched set: I in my workaday uniform of business suit and heels, Miguel in leather and tall boots, his jet-black hair slicked back. For the first time, I was a little embarrassed to be seen with him.

"Why don't you go on home now?" I said. "I'm going to work the rest of the day, there isn't anything for you to do here."

"You're going to *work*, querida? Why would you do that? I thought you were just here to pick up your stuff."

"No, I've got things on my desk that need to get done, and then I'll think about giving my two-week' notice."

"Give notice? You're loco. What do you care what gets done? You'll never work here again, or anywhere else. You're rich!"

I didn't bother to reply. That, in a nutshell, was why Miguel could never keep a job more than a few months. I thought of Maya Angelou's advice: when people show you who they are, believe them.

~*~

I didn't close my eyes one minute last night. Miguel slept, snoring and snorting like a pig. I don't think he'd smoke so much dope if he knew how he looks and sounds while he's sleeping it off. But, on the other hand, nothing could convince Miguel he's ever anything but beautiful.

When the first gray glimpse of morning illuminated the bedroom window, I slipped out of bed quietly and tiptoed from the room. The apartment was cold at that early hour, but I felt like I was burning up. The thought of all those dollars with my name on them generated its own heat. I made a cup of tea and carried it to the window overlooking the parking lot. The cars below were barely discernible in the dim light. If I closed my eyes and listened to the scrappy city birds tuning up for the new day, I could almost believe I was somewhere else, somewhere down a gravel lane, in a farmhouse set among fields of golden wheat.

I was urban to the core, raised in the shadow of skyscrapers. I'd always lived in close proximity to neighbors and stores and pavement. Yet I felt such affinity for my country's wide heartland and its distinctive music. The pathos and humor and honesty of that music echoed in my soul. I could count the number of Latina country artists on my fingers, but oh, how I wanted to be one of them.

This is my chance. All these years I've been saying if only I had the money I could go to Nashville, get discovered, be a country star. Well, now I've got the money. No excuses. I'm scared to death. For the millionth time, I wish I had a family. Here, in this country.

Mama and Papa came across the border illegally before I was born, leaving behind my brother and sister with la abuela. It must have been heart-wrenching for my devoted parents to leave their children, but they had their eyes on a better future and they knew that would not be in Mexico.

Education, that's what they wanted for their kids, and a fighting chance. And so they came, two among millions who somehow found their way across the miles of desert, through spiny cactus, over treacherous rivers, under blazing sun, past the armed border guards. They braved hunger and thirst and sickness just to get here, a place where nobody wanted them, knowing they could always land in jail instead of the promised land. All that, just for a chance at a better life for their family.

Mama and Papa took any jobs they could find, two or three apiece: yard work, house cleaning, baby-sitting, picking crops, carpet manufacturing, and worst of all, chicken processing. My mother always shuddered when she talked about the poultry plant. It was unrelentingly hard, but still so much easier than their life in Mexico that they considered themselves blessed. Eventually, they saved enough to pay a coyote to smuggle in my brother and sister. And then they had me, the anchor baby, the only legal American in the family.

Our home was steeped in Mexican culture. I remember the music, the loud, blaring mariachi that Papa loved. The aromas from the kitchen: spices and browning onions and simmering tomato sauce; just a hint of them makes my mouth water to this day. I remember the warmth of my mother's hands when she braided my long, black hair. Most of all, I remember the day the ICE agents came to the house and arrested everybody but me. I was eighteen.

It was a Saturday morning, and my brother and sister were at home, too, making the agents' haul worthwhile. They were not given time to grab a handbag or a jacket; my brother went barefooted. He had just gotten up.

"What should I do?" I screamed as my family was being hustled into the ICE van.

"Stay here, Bella," my papa called back to me. "Stay with the neighbors. We'll be in touch as soon as we can."

"Papa, Mama!"

But the van's slamming doors and revving engine drowned out my words. They were gone. Our old neighbor, Mrs. Montez, put her arms around me there in the street as I cried and cried.

"Vamanos, vamanos," she murmured, propelling me gently into her house. In our neighborhood, it wasn't wise to make a public scene. You never knew what it might draw down upon you.

My parents called when they got back to their home village in Mexico. Even after such a short separation, their voices sounded different.

"Hola, Bella?" my Mama said very loudly.

I smiled, because I knew she couldn't believe that telephones really worked at such a distance unless she shouted. As we talked, she kept throwing in Spanish words. It was as if her English had been planted in stony soil, and the hot sun of Mexico was drying it up. It made her seem foreign, somehow.

She told me they were all living with my Mama's family and it was very crowded. My brother and sister were looking for work, but there were not many jobs to be found in the little village, and maybe they would have to go to Mexico City.

When my Papa got on the line, he sounded beaten and very old.

"Should I come there, Papa? Should I come to you?"

"No, no. There is nothing for you here. Stay in school, my Niña," he said. "For you to go to college and graduate -- that is all I have left to hope for."

I couldn't bring them back to the United States, but I could give them that much, at least: I could stay in school. It became my mission.

In the days ahead, I cleaned out our house, keeping only a family portrait, my desk and my mother's rosary. I boxed up and shipped my family's clothing to their new address in Mexico, and sold everything else to help pay my way. *No crying, no crying, no crying*, I repeated dully to myself as I worked. When the house was empty, so was I. I turned the key over to the landlord and moved in with Mrs. Montez.

She was a kind old lady and never let on it was hard to suddenly have a teenage boarder interrupt her peaceful days. She gave me a little room under the eaves in her attic, her only spare room, broiling hot in summer and icily cold in winter. The mattress on my single bed was thin, but it was piled high with Mrs. Montez's beautiful homemade quilts. With my little desk from home and a few hooks that served as my closet, it was enough. There I could study uninterrupted late into the night, swatting away the fat bugs determined to squash themselves against my desk lamp.

I had a job, of course, everyone in our family did, and I continued working in the bodega after graduation. I saved almost my entire paycheck. Mrs. Montez refused to take a penny for my room and board, saying she was honored to help a girl so clearly on her way up. I tried to pay her back by cleaning her house every Saturday after work, helping in her little backyard garden and buying groceries. I didn't know it was possible to be so lonely.

My high school counselor took a special interest in me. She helped me get an academic scholarship to the junior college nearby and the following September I started classes. When I completed two years of junior college, I moved seamlessly on to the university on a scholarship. I was offered a dorm room in exchange for being a Resident Advisor. I worked in the cafeteria for my food, and cleaned cages in the dog lab for a little spending money.

Those years I was a robot: work, class, study. Work, class, study. I didn't dare dwell on feeling lonely and I couldn't afford to spend money on fun like my fellow students, so work was a great distraction. There were boys who asked me out and I dated a few of them, but I didn't allow myself to be deterred from my purpose. There would be plenty of time for boys after I had my degree. Later, later, I told myself.

Of course, I kept in touch with my family. I sent a little money when I could and we talked on my cell phone every weekend.

"Will you ever come back here?" I asked.

"No, Bella, we are too old to go through that again," my Papa said. "Things are better here now that your brother and sister are on their own. They help us when they can, and so do you. We get by.

Some day you will come here to visit and tell us all about your good American life."

I promised I would, but it never happened. When my brother called with the news that our parents were gone, dead in an epidemic of influenza that swept their village, taking the old ones and the babies, it was too late.

"Don't come for the funerals," he said. "Don't spend the money you need for school. More than anything, they wanted you to stay in school."

So I didn't go. Because I didn't see their bodies, didn't witness their joint funeral and the two coffins lowered side by side into the arid Mexican graveyard, my parents stayed alive to me. I often forgot they were no longer at the other end of the phone and dialed their number. A couple of times, I purchased money orders and sent them off as I had always done. My brother finally told me to stop.

"We won't take your money, Bella, and our parents no longer need it."

I heard the resentment in his voice. I had become the rich, insensitive gringa sister, a stranger to them. Gradually, we communicated less frequently until it was only cards at holidays and presents for my nieces and nephews on their birthdays.

But now -- now that I had money, I could do for them what others had done for me -- give them a boost into the middle class. Perhaps my brother and sister would be glad to know me again. I held no grudge. I would share my good fortune with them, with *familia.* What else is there, in the end?

I think that's why I fell so hard for Miguel. He

was Mexican, like me, like familia. He understood things about me that my American friends did not. I was homesick for a home I never knew, a culture I had absorbed only second-hand, a family that seemed to have forgotten me. Miguel embodied what I longed for and so I forgave him his pot-smoking, his lazy, manana attitude.

But even before the lottery win, Miguel's appeal was fading. Maybe I was growing up. If there was to be a male in my life, I wanted one who had something to contribute besides sex. A grown man instead of a boy.

I knew Miguel would insist on coming along to Nashville, and I didn't want him there with me. I anticipated a struggle. Miguel didn't like to give up what he considered his. Everything I knew about him suggested that he wouldn't take it gracefully when I told him we were through, especially now that I was suddenly very rich.

Scott

Getting that money! It was like the roller coaster climb when you go up, up, up, and the coaster is creaking and you wonder if it will hold together, and then -- *swoosh!* -- you're going faster than you've ever gone in your life, you're screaming and holding on tight -- and you're still wondering if it will hold together.

In a New York minute, I had trusts and stocks and annuities for the kids' college and loads of cash in several checking accounts. I quit my job immediately. In fact, I didn't even bother to quit, I just stopped going to work. Left all my personal stuff -- the spare white shirt from Wal-Mart, the dental floss and comb and Tums -- all of it in my bottom desk drawer. Let the next sucker clean it out, I didn't care.

Staying home with Jessie and the kids all day was not my idea of bliss. In true Jessie- style, she had a list of about a thousand things to do and I wasn't in any kind of mood to do them.

I had my own agenda. I had to consult with my lawyer, the honorable pipsqueak Lawrence Bickler, about my divorce. And I was house-hunting for my soon-to-be bachelor quarters. My realtor and Bickler both had strict orders never to call me at home. I planned to present Jessie with a done deal. I'd just leave one day like I was running an errand or something, and then have the sheriff's deputy serve her with the divorce papers. She'd probably freak out when I didn't come home that night, but I didn't want to hang around to hear her weeping and wailing. Take the easy way and take it fast.

I got a new wardrobe. My old clothes could hang in my closet until Jessie threw them out. They didn't suit my new lifestyle anyway. I had some suits tailor-made, although now that I wasn't working I had little need for them. Got my hair cut at the fanciest place in town, had my teeth whitened and visited a tanning booth until I attained a deep, rich-guy glow. Lost a few pounds, too. Yeah, I looked good.

Even though I wasn't quite ready to move out, I started my search for a new place. I didn't look long before settling on a big house by the lake, complete with a boat and dock. It was an impulse buy, but so what. I had no patience with trailing around looking at house after house; that's more a Jessie thing. With the promise of cash, the homeowner became motivated to close the deal immediately and to leave everything, including linens, pots and pans and a sleek speedboat. I couldn't be bothered shopping for all that stuff.

I didn't breathe a word about the new house to her. It was part of my Great Escape and my secret. I spent a lot of time there and Jessie didn't say a word about my absences from home or my improved appearance. In fact, she didn't do much talking at all, which was highly unusual for her. A couple of days she seemed sick – white-faced and shaky -- but I thought it was just more pregnancy drama. I didn't want to get sucked into all that, so I didn't ask. I guess I should have suspected something.

I bought that new car, by the way. It was a Porsche instead of a Jaguar. The woman who sold it to me, Ellen, threw in another freebie - herself. It must be true that money is a great aphrodisiac because *she* came on to *me*. I would never have dared aim so high -- women who look like Ellen don't usually pay any attention to married municipal clerks. Only I'm not that guy anymore, and Ellen really liked my money. It took me some time to get the new dynamics through my head.

It was the first time I'd ever been unfaithful to Jessie. I'd had lots of fantasies, but never the opportunity to act on them. I couldn't believe my luck. Ellen would come over for a quickie during her lunch hour, or she'd pick up food after she got off work and spend the evening at my new place. She got a little bitchy about picking up food, though.

"Geez, Scott, can't we go out to dinner like normal people?"

"Not just yet," I said. "Until the divorce is final, I can't afford to be seen out in public with a girl like you. You're such a knock-out, baby, everybody would be looking."

But my attempt at flattery fell flat.

"We could drive to another town," Ellen said, "I happen to know that you've got a new Porsche."

Funny, I hadn't noticed before that her voice could take on that whiney edge. I won about the dinners, but there were other things, too. Demands and requests and complaints – it got to be a pain, to be honest, and not too different from what I was used to at home, only without Jessie's leavening sweetness. So the affair was great fun and then it wasn't. And the bad ending? Well, maybe I'll get better at endings, too.

The day before the divorce papers were to be served, I left the house early, as usual. Jessie had no idea I had just spent the last night in our home and the last night as her husband. She didn't ask me where I was going, so I didn't have to make up any stories.

I went to my new place and was fooling around with the boat, basking in the sunshine, loving the slap of the waves against my -- *my!* -- dock, when a car pulled into the driveway. No one knew I'd bought the place, so I assumed it was friends of the former owner who didn't know he'd moved, or a salesman or maybe even Ellen, with a change of heart. But it was a deputy sheriff who got out of the car and approached me.

"Mr. Holmes? Scott Holmes?" he said.

"Yeah, what's up?"

He slapped some papers into my hand. "You've been served," he said as he turned and walked rapidly back to his car.

"Served what?" I asked stupidly.

A rapid perusal of the document revealed that Jessica Anne Holmes was suing Scott Allen Holme for divorce. A closer reading said that she was asking for half of all property, including my recent acquisitions, the house and boat. How did she know?

CHAPTER SIX

Marilyn

It was hard, trying to fit outside appointments into my regular work days. One of the things I really needed to do was get an attorney, and Star and Rowan kindly accompanied me to the offices of Bickler, Standers and Fraine. Young Mr. Bickler seemed to be the hero of the hour for snagging some wealthy clients. It was nice to be treated with such deference and respect. I began to get a feel for how life was changing.

Mom still couldn't grasp what my lottery win meant, no matter how slowly and patiently I explained it to her. She'd nod her head and say, "Uh huh, isn't that nice, dear," but I could tell she wasn't getting it. Her world was very small: our house, what she could see from the window in her bedroom, and our few remaining relatives, all as ancient as she, seldom seen because of the formidable logistics involved. She lived on her memories. The past was her reality.

I had to decide what to do about work. I'd been with the city government almost my entire working life and it was unimaginable to think of leaving. What would a whole, long, empty day be like? And yet, I no longer needed the paycheck and Mom needed me at home. (Or needed someone -- I kept forgetting I could pay for the very best home care now.) I made an appointment with my boss to talk it over.

Janna was much younger than I, promoted right over my head a couple of years ago. I didn't resent it. I knew I wasn't a good candidate for the job because of my obligations at home. I liked Janna, although she could be rather short-spoken at times. I was prepared to be magnanimous about working as long as I was needed. At the appointed time, I left my cubicle and presented myself in Janna's office. Her smooth blonde head was bent toward her computer screen in rapt concentration and she left me standing there for a minute before she looked up, removed her glasses and invited me to sit. Then she took the lead in our conversation.

"I assume you're giving me your notice, Marilyn," she said, foregoing small talk.

"Well, I hadn't thought...."

"We were surprised that you even showed up the next day after we heard of your lottery win," Janna continued. "But we certainly understand that you are now ready to leave the working world."

"I haven't gotten very far in my planning," I said. "I could stay on until you find someone and then train that person."

"No need. We're going to give your job to Anita. Actually, we're going to combine your job and hers, which she can easily handle, so it will be a cost-saving for the department."

"Oh." Losing me, after all these years, was actually a cost-saver? Roll my job into Anita's, *which she can easily handle*? Not only was I not a valued employee, I was doing them a favor by leaving.

"So here's your hat, what's your hurry?" I said, trying to cover my hurt feelings with a joke.

"Now, Marilyn, don't take offense. You're nearing retirement anyway, and naturally, as a manager, I have to plan ahead. You have the opportunity now to just enjoy the time you have left."

The time I have left? Why, you arrogant little snot! I'd once watched a mother robin push the last, reluctant fledgling out of the nest. Now I knew exactly how that little bird felt: unready, unsure and airborne anyway. I also remembered that it flapped its wings and flew. I stood.

"It sounds like you're all set," I said, trying to make my voice as crisp and unemotional as Janna's. "I think I'll just go on right now."

"Of course, we'll want to plan some kind of retirement party for you," Janna said, already stealing a glance at her computer screen.

"No thanks. Mother and I are leaving almost immediately; we're planning to spend some time in Italy," I said, improvising wildly. "After all, we need to enjoy the time we have left."

Janna had the grace to redden. I turned without another word and went to my desk where I quickly cleared my few personal belongings from the drawers. My co-workers seemed oblivious to my preparations for departure, even when I rummaged around the copy room and came out carrying a cardboard box. My best work friend was out that day; surely if she'd been in the office, there would have been some kind of acknowledgement. Had I always been so unimportant? I packed my stuff, put the desk key in an envelope with Janna's name on it and left it in the center of the blotter. And then I just walked out. No one even looked up from their work to see me leave.

So much for thirty years of loyal service and what I thought were genuine friendships. As I drove my car down the familiar ramp of the employee parking deck for the last time, an unexpected wave of euphoria hit me. I was free! I'd never been free, ever, in my entire life. I couldn't wait to see what would happen next.

~*~

I stopped on the way home and bought flowers for Mom. Just grocery store tulips, but pink, her favorite color. They would look pretty on her bedside table. I wanted to soften the surprise of having me come home in the middle of the afternoon with news of my new, jobless state.

"Mom, it's me," I called as I entered the house through the kitchen door.

There was no answer. She must be napping, I thought, and began tiptoeing. I filled a small green luster ware pitcher with water for the tulips and I carried them with me to Mom's room. Peeking around the open door, I saw her lying on her bed. She was fully dressed, just as I'd left her that morning before I went to work. I started to withdraw, but something in the quality of her stillness made me pause.

"Mom? Wake up, Mom. I'm home early."

Nothing. I crossed the room to her bedside, depositing the flowers on her nightstand. Her eyes were open just a slit. So she *is* awake, I thought. Ill? I touched her shoulder, which felt oddly immobile under my hand.

"Mom?" I said again.

But by then I knew she would not answer. Would never answer again. I sat down beside her and took her hand, already cool, in mine.

"Oh, Mom. You're gone."

I didn't cry, not then. What I felt was too deep for easy tears. My mother was the constant in my life. There was never a time when we didn't live together, never a time when I didn't know that she loved me unconditionally. Since I hadn't married, she remained my north star long after most women transferred their primary allegiance to husbands and children.

The last years of her illness were hard, but her sweet spirit kept us both from getting bitter about the burdens of old age. Now it felt natural and right that she had died as quietly as she had lived. I knew I'd grieve for my loss, for my loneliness, but I wouldn't grieve for Mom's life, so limited by illness and age. After a while, I got up and went back to the kitchen, where I called the police.

When a death occurs at home, that's what you do; you call the police. I didn't call 911 because it wasn't an emergency. I spoke to a receptionist who answered at the police department's main number and told her my mother had passed away. She sounded puzzled.

"Hang up and dial 911," she said.

"But there's no emergency, she just died in her sleep. I don't know what to do next, but I read somewhere that the police should be notified about a home death."

"Hang up and call 911," she said again, a tinge of impatience in her voice.

So I did and in just a few minutes I heard the sirens. First an enormous red fire truck pulled into our driveway and several fully uniformed firefighters with medical bags in hand jumped out and ran for the house. I opened the door to them and showed them back to Mom's bedroom. They examined her, pulling up her eyelids to shine a light in her eyes and holding a stethoscope to her silent chest.

"Ma'am, I'm sorry to inform you that your mother -- is this your mother? -- it appears your mother has passed away," one of them said.

"I know. That's why I called. I don't need--" I heard another siren approach and went back to the front door to admit the paramedics. They went through the same motions as the fire fighters had and then we all agreed that my mother was indeed dead.

By then I felt a terrible urge to laugh. It was like those times in childhood when you're in church or at a funeral and you get the giggles, knowing that it's totally inappropriate and you're going to be in big trouble, but you can't stop. I excused myself and went into the bathroom where I stared sternly into my own eyes in the mirror until the moment passed.

When I returned to the bedroom, the paramedics were loading Mom's body onto a stretcher. Someone had closed her eyes. When she was securely strapped down, a white sheet was pulled up over her head. That's the first time it felt real - when I could no longer see her face. I walked beside her when she left our home for the last time.

"We'll take her to the medical examiner's office, Ma'am," one the paramedics said. "That's standard procedure for a home death. Here is a card with the phone number. You can call, or have your funeral director call, to find out when the body can be released."

I nodded dumbly, and noticed for the first time that all the neighbors were standing outside watching. Their faces reflected curiosity, sadness, concern, sympathy. I couldn't deal with them. I turned and hurried back into the house.

~*~

Like many old people who take a long time dying, Mom had planned her funeral down to the last detail. She'd chosen a mortuary and made arrangements with the director, prepaying everything. All I had to do was follow the instructions she'd left neatly filed with her will. Before I fully comprehended my loss, I was standing at an open grave beside my father's tombstone, listening while the minister said the last words over my mother's coffin. I placed a bunch of pink tulips on the lid. Then I left. I didn't want to see the coffin's descent into the ground.

My house had been invaded while I was gone. The smell of casseroles greeted me at the door, and in the kitchen was enough food for a family to live on for a week. Why is it that death provokes a feast? Neighbor women were filling glasses and dishing up plates, seemingly as at home in my kitchen as their own. Mom's few remaining relatives, all ancient and tottering, came to the house after the funeral to be fed and comforted. Bella, Star, Rowan and Darren were there, too, passing trays, washing dishes, refilling glasses and, finally, locating canes and purses and helping the old mourners gently out to their cars. Then, one by one, my friends and neighbors patted my shoulder, murmured a few sympathetic words and slipped out the kitchen door.

I was alone. I remembered my feeling of freedom as I'd left city hall for the last time. Janis Joplin's raw voice looped through my head: "Freedom's just another word for nothing left to lose." I had a lot of money, but nothing left to lose.

There was a lot to do. I went to the medical examiner's office and picked up the death certificate: natural causes was the official verdict. Copies had to be mailed to the Social Security office, Medicare and Dad's pension administrator, letting them know to stop the benefits. Mom's will was filed with the court and placed in probate -- a joke, really, since she had almost nothing left and what little she did have came to me, her only child.

I resolutely cleaned her closet and bureau drawers, putting her familiar, worn nightgowns and robes into garbage bags. They weren't good enough to donate. I kept the books, her favorite soft pink sweater and her eyeglasses. Nothing seems more personal than eyeglasses, somehow. Goodwill picked up her bedroom furniture and recliner. I hired a painter -- pre-lottery, I would have done it myself -- to paint the walls a neutral ivory color. Her old room was now an empty box. I closed the door.

And now what? I asked myself. No job, no mother to care for, no chick nor child. Oh, money, sure, lots of money. But what to do with it and with myself? I'd told Janna that mother and I were going to Italy, and I considered going alone now. But I'd never traveled abroad in my life, didn't have a passport, and didn't speak Italian -- it just seemed too hard. I discovered that even money isn't much fun when there's no one to share it with.

There's nothing like self-pity to bring on the tears, and I shed them in great abundance. I wasn't mourning my mother so much as I was feeling very sorry for Marilyn. It was unattractive, to say the least, and not much fun, but maybe it was a necessary step in dealing with my new reality.

Pure and simple, I was lonely. Days that had been full of work and then caring for Mom were now empty and endless. I'd never dated much, even as a teenager. There was one special man in my life when I was twenty-five, but our affair didn't last long and my heart wasn't as broken as I thought it should be when he ended it.

It would be a wonderful thing to have a

companion, someone to help me figure out how to spend my money and share in the enjoyment of it. But where would a sixty-something stay-at-home woman meet eligible men?

Darren

Rowan was right when he predicted that I had more friends and relatives than I knew. The phone rang continuously. Finally I had the land line disconnected and got new cell phones for Mom and me.

Mom was barely speaking to me. Of all the reactions I might have predicted, I never imagined she'd be so sad. What kind of mother is sad when her son wins the lottery? She wouldn't even discuss it with me. The air was loaded with tension, making it hard to draw a deep breath.

I turned in my two weeks' notice at work. Old habits die hard, so even though I would never need another job or a reference for one, I had no wish to leave on bad terms. I dutifully trained my replacement. It wasn't an easy time. I came to dread every elevator ride, every coffee break and every e-mail from my co-workers for fear there would be another request for money. I heard about this one's sick child, that one's foreclosed house, another's sure-fire business venture that only needed capital. It was disheartening to keep saying no, no, no. Thank God I had taken Rowan's advice about tying the money up from the get-go so it wasn't available for loans. I think I could have given away my whole $18 million just in the office. I did quietly hand out some small amounts of cash. I just couldn't help it.

The one person I felt I could talk to about it was Bella. She was still working, too, because she felt sorry for her boss and guilty about his laments over never finding a replacement as good as she was. She was having her own encounters with pleading co-workers.

Talking over lunch one day, she said, "I wish there was some way to take myself out of the equation when people need money. It would be a full-time job to triage the genuine need from the I-wanna's. I'd love to help some who've asked, but I don't want my new job to be The Decider."

"Bill Gates set up that foundation of his," I said, "and, while we aren't in his league, maybe we could do something similar on a smaller scale."

"You mean so people could ask for help from an *organization* instead of us, personally?"

"Yes. And what could be more helpful than scholarships?" I was thinking out loud. "We know all too well that government workers don't make a lot of money, at least not at our level. What if we could help our co-workers who are trying to figure out how to finance college or trade school for their kids?"

"Having a marketable skill makes all the difference in a person's life," Bella said. "Not everybody is college material but everyone can learn a trade. Plumbers, electricians, mechanics -- good ones are always in demand and they won't see their jobs outsourced overseas. Yet I'm not aware that there are many trade school scholarships out there."

"How would we do it?" I asked. "It sounds like

a full-time job to set parameters, take applications, screen applicants, monitor progress, write checks, keep the books-- I don't know about you, but that sounds like work, which is what we are trying to get away from."

"We'd definitely need an administrator. And we should give the others a chance to participate. I feel sure Star would want to contribute and she might have some good ideas about how to set it up, drawing from her experience with Section Eight housing."

"I doubt if Scott will be interested, but I bet Marilyn will. If four of us establish a big-enough endowment, it can keep funding itself from investment earnings."

"Yes, and we'd have somebody else to make the decisions, take ourselves out of it except for the funding part. It would be a good tax write-off for us," Bella said. "Should we confine it to city employees and their families?"

"I think so, or we'll get a tsunami of applications from all over the place. Let's talk to Lawrence. His law firm probably has somebody with expertise in this area."

Everyone reacted with enthusiasm except Scott. I didn't care -- to hell with him -- but it was important to Star that we were united in establishing the foundation. She called us all together to discuss it, with the unstated but apparent hope that we could convince him to join us.

"It's a way to give back," she said. "I know that's a cliché, but I think it would send a good message if we do this together."

"Good message to who?" Scott asked, his lip curled.

"I don't know. Karma? Don't you want to help people you know who are still in the same difficulties you've left behind?"

"Nope."

"But Scott -- think of what it will mean. Kids will be able to get an education who otherwise couldn't. You might be training the mechanic who fixes that fancy car of yours. Or a doctor who saves your life someday."

"Oh, please," Scott said. "Let them win their own lottery. I'm not interested."

That was that. We went ahead without him. Lawrence Bickler launched himself enthusiastically into the groundwork. Say what you will about Scott, one thing he got right was finding us an attorney. Larry was a gem.

Bickler, Standers and Fraine did indeed have an attorney on staff with experience in non-profit foundations, and he took over with reassuring authority. We all felt relieved to be able to include others in some of our good fortune; apparently at least four of us had taken to heart those early lessons about sharing.

Bella and I continued to meet and talk, sometimes at lunch or sometimes after work at a little pub around the corner. I drank Diet Cokes. I'd decided I could stand to lose a few pounds, and I was tired of waking up with a hang-over, so I ditched the vodka. Did I make that sound easy? It was hell. We tell ourselves, we drinkers on the way to being drunks, that it's just a social habit, we don't actually *need* the booze, we can stop whenever we choose. We lie. Late nights were the hardest times for me, a time of gauzy fatigue when I was accustomed to washing away the frustrations of the day on a tide of vodka. I started taking long walks instead, sneaking out of the house with my shoes in hand, just like a teenager, to avoid Mom's beady eye and relentless questions. The walks helped to reduce the craving and they also melted off the little drinker's belly I'd acquired. Finally, I began to feel better, then good, then so well that I realized I'd been living in a fog. My newfound health was something money couldn't buy, but I doubt if I'd ever have achieved it had I not been prodded out of my corner by all those greenbacks.

Bella noticed. "Good for you," was all she said, and I felt myself blushing with pride. Her quiet praise felt like a medal pinned to my chest.

She was preoccupied with trouble of her own: Miguel.

"The relationship is over," she told me, "but he just won't accept it and move out. He cries and then I feel sorry and guilty and let him stay, but I'm beginning to hate him for it. We both need to move past this break-up and get on with our lives."

"Let's say, for the sake of argument, that Miguel really loves you, Bella, and genuinely hates to lose you. You gotta feel sorry for the guy. And now the money complicates things even more. Would you be willing to give him some of it to get rid of him?"

"It seems like such an ugly way to end our relationship, like I'm buying him off or something. I did love him once and I still care what happens to him."

She thought a moment. "I don't know how real his feelings are, but I bet he'd accept money. Maybe I'll try to talk to him about it and see what his reaction is."

We sat in silence for a few minutes. I had my own questions to mull over.

"Can you give me any insight into why Mom is giving me the silent treatment? She didn't want me to take the money, if you can imagine that. The atmosphere at home is like a wet week."

Bella took her time answering. That's one of the things I like about her, that thoughtful pause while she really thinks over what she's going to say.

"Maybe she's scared," Bella said. "She's afraid you'll move out and she'll be all alone. There's not enough money in the world to make up for that. And she's right, isn't she? It's way past time for you to be out on your own and now there's no excuse not to do it."

"Yeah, I'm thinking about it. I'm trying to give her a little time to get used to the idea."

"She may never get used to it. You can do everything possible to reassure her that you'll stay in her life, and make her financially comfortable. But the fact is, your lives are going to change -- have already changed. You can't control her reaction. It's up to her to deal with it."

Sometimes Bella is wise beyond her years.

CHAPTER SEVEN

Bella

It's hard to know who you can trust. There are very few people you can really talk to after you've won the lottery. It's a unique experience. Most people are envious and that makes some of them scornful and dismissive. Others want what you've got and you can see, behind their eyes, they are trying to figure out how to take it from you.

Surprisingly, Darren Davis turned out to be a confidant. We knew each other the way you know someone working in the same office, but our acquaintance didn't go beyond our joint venture in the lottery pool. I'd heard he still lived with his mother and was under her thumb, so I guess if I thought about him at all, I thought he was a loser. But being co-winners put a different spin on things. Darren was still working, too, so we began meeting for lunch or after work for a drink. We talked about investments and financial advisors, how to fend off people with their hands out, how to know whom to help, and then, inevitably, we got around to personal matters. Darren updated me about his Mom's depression since he told her about all the cash.

"I finally sat her down last night and we talked about what the money will mean in our lives. She thought I'd leave, go live some kind of Hugh Hefner life-style on the French Riviera, I guess. She was worried sick. I told her I do want to have my own place soon, and I hope to have a family one day. She said of course, she understood that, but she was afraid for me, afraid I'd fall in with bad companions. She actually said bad companions."

"In my case, I already have the bad companion," I said. "What am I going to do about Miguel?"

"If you don't love him, you are doing him no kindness by letting him linger," Darren said. "My Dad used to say that stringing out a difficult decision is like docking a puppy's tail by inches. God, where did he ever come up with such a blood-thirsty example?"

"But your dad was right, wasn't he? I've tried to break up with Miguel before and he carried on until I felt so guilty I'd drop it. He accused me of using him until I got rich and then ditching him, but the truth is, I knew our relationship was pretty well over before that winning ticket came along. I have to be firm with Miguel, no matter how pathetic he acts. I'm going to do it tonight."

I didn't waste a minute when I got home, telling Miguel we needed to talk. Does a woman ever say that when she has good news? He was stretched out on the couch, smoking a joint and eating Cheetos. He swung his feet down to the floor, sat up and gave me the lazy smile he thinks melts my heart.

"So, talk, querida. What's on your mind?"

Predictably, it did not go well. Miguel went through all the stages of grief in one conversation.

Denial -- "You can't mean it, querida!"

Anger -- "You think you can just toss me out like an old shoe? You're not tossing me nowhere! You'll be sorry for this."

Bargaining -- "I'll do whatever you say, I'll change, just tell me what you want."

Depression -- "My life is not worth living without you. There's nothing left for me now."

Finally, sulky acceptance -- "Fine! If you don't want me, I'll just go."

It was past midnight when he finally threw his t-shirts and socks in a duffle bag and stood at the door of my apartment.

"I don't know where I'll spend the night," he said, head down. "I guess I'll have to sleep in my car."

I guiltily stuffed some bills in his jacket pocket. He glared at me, black eyes flashing, but he kept the money.

I took a deep, deep breath after Miguel left. It felt like there was more air in the apartment. I hadn't realized how much oxygen our uneasy relationship was consuming.

~*~

Being free of Miguel gave me the emotional energy to be firm about turning in my notice at work and not wavering when my boss began moaning about finding a replacement.

"If you hurry, I'll still be here to train whoever you hire," I said. "But in two weeks, I'm out of here."

Personnel sent up three candidates the next day and the mayor chose one -- definitely not the one I'd have selected. Her name was Madonna but she had a gritty quality incompatible with holiness. Big of hair, bust and bum, she had the personality to match. Her reaction to my training was to argue about my methods, confident that the way *she'd* do it would work better. At first I felt sorry for her -- breaking in to a new job is tough -- but when I realized she believed herself to be slumming, my patience developed little holes through which my temper could escape.

"Look, Madonna," I said toward the middle of the week of training. "This is the way the mayor likes it done. Maybe when you've worked for him awhile and he trusts you, you can suggest trying it your way. Your way may turn out to be better. But for now, for God's sake, just humor me."

She looked at me, had enough sense to see that my teeth were gritted and there was a dangerous glint in my eyes, and nodded once. Okay. Once is a start.

If you've ever trained your replacement, you know how difficult it is to explain everything you do, including the tasks that are so routine they've become second nature. Nashville burned brighter and brighter on my horizon as we struggled through the days. After Madonna departed at five PM, I stayed on to finish up the work that I couldn't get done during the day.

I reflected with some bitterness on the easy life that wealth brings as I logged out of the computer and picked up my purse at nine PM one night. The lonely forays into the deserted parking deck were creeping me out. I wasn't exactly afraid, but I was hyper vigilant of my surroundings. A couple of times, I thought I caught a glimpse of a man on foot in the deck, but the figure was in the shadows and I couldn't be sure I'd even seen anyone. I hurried to my car and locked the doors as soon as I got inside.

I thought uneasily of Miguel, but I hadn't heard from him since he'd left my apartment. It seemed he'd finally accepted that we were over. I told myself it was in an abundance of caution that I had my apartment locks re-keyed. Now I had the only key that opened my door.

Darren and I had our last day in the office on the same day, and celebrated by going out for dinner after work. We were both feeling light-hearted with relief at having finally closed one phase of our lives. Our conversation ranged far and wide that evening.

"I really am going to Nashville now," I said. "I don't know one thing about how to break into the music business, so I'm just going to go to Tootsie's Orchid Lounge or somewhere like that, and see if I can wrangle a spot on open-mike night. Maybe somebody will hear me and -- I don't know, sometimes forward motion takes you to places you didn't even know were there."

"Well, that's as good a plan as any," Darren said. "I'm still trying to figure out my next move. I told Mom to start house-hunting but she said she didn't want to leave the house where she and Dad lived. So now I'm trying to convince her to let me spend some money on remodeling the place. You never saw anyone so reluctant to make changes, even good ones."

"That's why I want to seize my opportunities right now," I said, "before I get set in my ways."

Darren knew I'd been feeling jumpy lately and insisted on following me back to my apartment and walking me to the door after dinner. Although I protested that it wasn't necessary, I was glad for his presence. We were discussing new cars, an engrossing prospect now within reach for both of us, when I put my new key in the lock. But before I could turn it, the door swung open and only then did I notice the splintered door frame. Inside, my living room looked like it had been redecorated with a hatchet. The upholstered furniture bled stuffing from jagged cuts in the fabric. The carpet was soggy with what smelled like maple syrup. Broken glass was everywhere; pictures and books littered the floors and the curtains hung in crazy tatters. In the kitchen, the refrigerator door was open and most of the contents, including eggs, had been flung out on the floor.

The worst damage was in my bedroom. There were holes in the walls, my clothing was cut in pieces and strewn all over the room, and the mattress and box springs were slashed and soaked with urine. The stench made me gag. On the bathroom mirror there was a crude drawing done with my lipstick of a knife with blood spatters around it.

I turned to Darren in disbelief. It was such a bizarre scene that I hadn't yet found my tears.

"What should I do?" I asked. I could hear that I sounded like a child.

"Come on outside," Darren said, putting his arm around me and steering me toward the door. "Let's go sit in my car and call the police. You need to report this and then we'll figure out where you can spend the rest of the night."

"I want to go to Star's," I said.

Darren

Yes, that was a disappointment. In my mind, I imagined a very different scene, one in which Bella collapsed into my arms murmuring, "Hold me, Darren; I don't want to be alone." Obviously, she and I were not quite on the same relationship page. But now wasn't the time to press the issue; if she wanted to go to Star's house, then so be it.

I never expected to get close to someone like Bella. She was a glamorous figure in our little corner of the world, always poised and confident, whether sitting at the mayor's right hand in meetings or handling our constituents with tact and aplomb. Like the popular cheerleader in high school, she was intimidating to a nonentity like me. But after we won the lottery together, friendship followed naturally. It was I who wanted more, and it was my inexperience and sexual timidity that kept me from making a move. I saw Annie's face again. Had I not matured at all in the intervening seventeen years since I let her go?

When I saw Bella home that night, I was hoping she'd ask me in. We'd only been together in public places and I wanted to see her in her own home. I wanted to be her guest. But when we got to her apartment, the splintered door led us inside where we found the worst mess imaginable.

"Who would do this?" I asked, knowing it was a rhetorical question.

Bella just looked at me. Then she asked me to take her to Star's. My heart fell, but of course, that was exactly the right place for her. Star was everybody's mom and she took Bella in like a returning child. I went on home, sad that it wasn't me who was taking care of Bella. The evening had brought into sharp focus feelings I hadn't yet fully acknowledged to myself.

Bella

Star and Rowan reacted just right. Without asking questions, Star took me straight to her immaculate bathroom and ran a deep, hot bath scented with lavender. I soaked for a long time and thought about the men in my life.

Darren surprised me. I would never have imagined he could take charge so decisively and at the same time, treat me with such tenderness. It revealed a steadfast aspect of his character that I found very appealing. Up to now, I'd always been attracted to bad boys, and Miguel had been all flash and fury. Especially fury, as I had now witnessed, to my horror. What would I have done if I'd gone home alone and stepped into that awful mess? Or worse, arrived while he was creating it?

When I went downstairs in borrowed

pajamas, Rowan had a big bowl of hot, buttered popcorn waiting for me and I realized I was hungry. Star and Rowan made undemanding small talk, as if nothing could be more commonplace than me in their living room at 11 p.m., wearing pajamas and eating popcorn. Finally, I was ready to talk about it. "Of course, it was Miguel," I said.

"What did the police say?" Rowan asked.

"Not much. They wrote down my report and dusted for fingerprints. They said they'd have the door boarded shut when they were finished. I have renter's insurance so I'll file a claim first thing in the morning. Then I'll have to inform the apartment manager of the break-in and hire a cleaning crew, I guess."

"Do you have a place to stay? You know you are welcome here, for as long as you want," Star said. Rowan nodded.

"Thank you so much, both of you. But I won't impose on your hospitality after tonight. I'll get a hotel room and use it for a base while I figure out what I'm going to do next. This might be just the push I need to actually go to Nashville. There's nothing to keep me here, now."

The thought of making all those plans, replenishing my wardrobe from the skin out, dealing with the police and apartment management, and worst of all, looking over my shoulder for Miguel, suddenly seemed too much. The tears of weariness and shock found me then. *In the morning, I'll call Darren.*

~*~

It turned out I didn't need to call Darren because he was ringing Star's doorbell at 9 a.m., just as we were finishing breakfast. I was surprised at how glad I was to see him.

"Thought you could use some help today," he said shyly, accepting a steaming cup of coffee from Star. Rowan had left for work hours ago, so it was just us girls sitting around like the ladies of leisure we now were. Darren pulled up a chair and we began a list. I'm a great believer in lists when I'm faced with a big job, and rebuilding my life seemed very big indeed. Darren surprised me again with his organizational skills.

"You need clothes," he said.

"That's for sure. I'll go to Macy's at the mall and get the basics. Once I have enough clothing to get me through a week, I can relax and add to my wardrobe when I can have fun doing it. It won't be fun to shop right now; I've got too many other pressing matters to deal with. So shopping will be Number Two on the list."

"The first thing to be done is contact your apartment manager," Darren said. "One of your neighbors may have already reported the break-in to the front office, so it's important that you get in touch. Have you decided what you want to do about moving?"

I told him about staying in a hotel while I made plans to go to Nashville.

"I don't ever want to live in that apartment again, but I don't know whether the break-in would be grounds for terminating my lease," I said. "It still has a year to run."

"And what's the worst thing that could happen if you break your lease?" Darren asked, his eyes twinkling.

"Why, I'd have to pay the rest of..." I stopped, grinning sheepishly.

"Exactly!"

We laughed, the three of us, at how easy it was to forget that we were rich. Darren ticked down the list: see apartment manager and break lease; shop for clothes; book hotel room for indefinite stay; meet Darren for dinner.

I looked at him, eyebrows raised, as I read the last item.

"Unless you want me to spend the day with you?" he said. "I'd be happy to drive you around."

"That would help. I'd like that," I said. "Give me thirty minutes."

Darren

Bella and I checked off all the items on the list, first visiting her apartment manager to report the break-in and vandalism of her place. The manager was only too eager to terminate her lease in return for no trouble about the complex's security, or lack thereof. Bella paid him to hire a crew to clean out her apartment.

"I'll go and pick up a few personal things, photo albums and books. As for the rest, keep whatever you want, dump it, give it away, sell it, I don't care," she said. "Most of it is trash now. I never want to see it again."

Then I took Bella shopping. Ordinarily, I'd have to be hog-tied and gagged, then dragged bodily, leaving a bloody trail into a lady's clothing department. But because I was with Bella, I followed along like a lamb. I remembered my high-school sweetheart, dear Annie, and how we were joined at the hip, following each other in the most mind-numbing activities just so we could be together. I'd come full circle.

It turned out to be fairly painless. Bella went through Macys like a dose of salts. A bemused saleswoman and I followed in her wake, arms outstretched to accept the clothing she pulled from the racks. She tried on nothing.

"I know my size. If something doesn't fit, I'll return it."

She got seven of everything -- jeans, shirts, jackets, and shoes. A couple of dresses and skirts joined the pile now deposited beside the saleswoman's cash register.

"Okay, you sit here and wait for me," Bella ordered, dumping her purse in my lap as she entered the lingerie department alone. I exchanged commiserating glances with another guy who was holding a purse. Clearly, we communicated silently, we are just being very, very nice. Clearly, we'd rather be someplace manly. But part of me was secretly thrilled to be there with Bella.

She came back carrying more bags and pronounced our expedition over. We made our way back to the car and headed downtown.

"Where to?" I asked.

"Let's make it the Ritz."

Not only did she make it the Ritz, she made it a suite.

"What the heck?" she said in response to my dropped jaw. "I can afford it, remember? I can even afford to open the mini bar!"

Open it she did, and we upended several of those harmless-looking little bottles. Since I'd stopped the nightly vodka drinking, I got buzzed fairly fast. Bella, too, was looking a little loose around the edges.

"Darren!" she said solemnly. "You're the pest frien' -- no, I mean the best frien' -- I ever had."

"You're a good friend, too."

"Come here and let me give you a big hug."

But by the time I untangled my feet and made it across the room, she'd turned to look out the window at the panoramic view of downtown, all lit up for the night. We were fairly well lit-up for the night ourselves, but it seemed rude to grab her when her attention had clearly wandered.

"I think I'll jush shake a shower," she said, heading for the bathroom.

"I'll wait for you downstairs."

Regretfully, cursing myself for being a gentleman and an idiot, I let myself out of her room and took the elevator down to the lobby. I reflected dolefully that at least I wasn't so low that I'd take advantage of a drunk girl. What a guy. I found a deep chair behind a large plant and had a little snooze.

Bella found me and woke me with a shake. She looked fresh as a spring morning with no sign that those little bottles had been upended. I felt like a mile of dirt road, but managed to pull myself together and escort her into the Ritz dining room for dinner. Bella was ready to make a new plan and that plan included Nashville.

"I'll go with you if you like," I said, holding my breath as I awaited her reply.

"Thank you, Darren. I appreciate that, I really do. But I think I need to go alone. This is my chance to prove myself. I think it might be easier if there's nobody from home to see me if I fall on my face."

"What if you don't fall on your face? What if they love you in Nashville and you turn out to be a big country star? Will you remember your old friends then?"

"What do you think?"

Bella's smile could convince me of anything. Later I realized she'd made no promises.

CHAPTER EIGHT

Scott

I slid into the driveway, tires screeching, left the car door swinging open and hit the front door at a dead run.

"Jessie!" I roared, "Jessie, you better get in here."

"Right here, Scott," Jessie said, standing calmly in the kitchen doorway. "And don't worry, the kids are at my Mom's. I knew you'd come right over and you'd be angry."

"What the hell are you playing at?" I yelled, waving the divorce papers in her face. "What kind of sneaking, conniving bitch are you?"

"You're upset because I beat you to it, but we both know you were going to serve me with divorce papers tomorrow."

"How do you know that? And how do you know about my investments and the new house? And what the hell makes you think you're going to get half of my money?"

"I had a visit from Ellen," Jessie said. "Remember her, your ex-girlfriend? She had a lot of information she wanted to share. You really should have given her the loan she asked for. It would have been cheaper in the long run."

Ellen! "You can't believe anything that cheap whore had to say," I began. But Jessie cut me off.

"I'm way past believing or not believing, Scott. I *know* what you've been up to. Ellen told me all about the new house and boat and car. You're not nearly as good at deception as you think you are, and you're not the only one who is capable of planning ahead. I have to look out for not only myself but for Katie and Daniel and the little one I'm carrying."

This was a new Jessie. No tears or quavering voice; she didn't look scared or sorry and she certainly wasn't trying to please me. I wanted to strangle her. I was amazed at how much I wanted to put my hands around her neck and squeeze and squeeze. I flexed my fingers with the need. She noticed.

"I'm not afraid of you, if that's what you're hoping for. My Dad's in the back yard and he brought his shotgun. Remember how much he loves to hunt? He's a dead shot, never misses. He can be with us in a minute.

"Let me tell you how it's going to be," she continued. "I'm going to have this baby and raise our kids and I'm going to do it on your money. You can be part of their lives or not, it's up to you. After they are grown, I don't ever want to see you or hear your name."

"Oh, and I guess I get no say in the matter, huh, Jessie?" I layered as much sarcasm into my voice as possible.

"You do have an option."

"Really! Well, enlighten me. What is my option?"

"You can do it the hard way or the easy way. If you want to give your lawyer a big bag of money and go through the publicity of a court trial, that's fine with me. I'll ask for a jury. Let's see...who would be a more sympathetic figure; the lottery winner who is ditching his family or the pregnant mother of two little ones?"

I stared at her. Where was the compliant girl I'd married? The one who cried if she thought I was displeased... the one who never said no to sex, and never complained about being pregnant three times in four years. A change in tactics was called for.

"Hey, Jessie, honey, of course I got mad," I said, trying a rueful smile. "I never thought you'd go behind my back. It was a shock, that's all, but I understand where you're coming from. And of course I want you and the children to have everything you need. I just want some time on my own to... to work through all the changes that have come into my life."

"Poor little rich boy," Jessie said with a smile that looked genuinely amused.

I tried putting the hate I felt into my eyes. That always got to her. But she kept smiling as she returned my gaze. Then she turned and walked away.

Jessie

Jessie went to college with a goal -- a nursing

degree -- and she took it seriously. Knowing what her parents were sacrificing to get her through school kept her focused. She had an occasional date, maybe two with the same guy, but no more. Then she met Scott.

A mutual friend introduced them casually at a mundane Friday night gathering: "Jessie, meet Scott. Scott, Jessie." The friend didn't seem to notice that the air around them crackled. They were a couple from that night on. She finished nursing school with a much lower grade average than she'd hoped for, thanks to all those wonderful late nights with Scott, and they married the weekend after graduation. She was a real nurse at the local hospital and he was a newly-minted city accountant. Their life together -- their real life -- had begun.

The first year was a little rough. Jessie read the articles in women's magazine saying it was to be expected as couples adjusted to married life and adult responsibilities. Scott seemed distracted at times and unpredictably angry. He spoke to her in a hard, impatient voice she'd never heard when they were dating. She tried harder to please him.

~*~

"Scott! The test is positive. We're pregnant."

She could hardly speak for excitement, waving the home-pregnancy test stick joyfully as she emerged from the bathroom. They'd just had their first anniversary and secretly she'd been hoping for a baby, hoping a baby would make things right again.

"*We* are?" Scott said. "Guess I'll have to shop for bigger pants."

That was all. Later, he said some of the right things and made a visible effort to drum up some enthusiasm, but Jessie never forgot his spontaneous reaction to the news of their impending first child.

Trying to please an indifferent person is a wearisome, heart-deadening task, but Jessie tried. She made it a point to always say yes to whatever Scott wanted; never complained of being tired or discouraged or angry; took pains with her appearance. After Scott bitched about helping with the household chores, she went to part-time at work. He came home to a clean house, children bathed and ready for bed, and the aroma of supper cooking: all the things the books and women's magazines advised.

But it didn't seem to matter to him one way or another. He never acknowledged her efforts, although he was quick to complain of the inconvenience a sick child or an appliance suddenly gone rogue. Marriage wasn't turning out to be what she'd hoped for, but maybe that was her fault. In any case, she didn't know what else to do to fix it.

The lottery win seemed to open new doors. Surely now, with plenty of money and no financial worries, Scott would relax. He spent a lot of time away from home and didn't bother to hide his boredom when he was there, but maybe he just needed to adjust. Beneath her attempts at positive thinking, Jessie knew whatever was wrong was deeply wrong. Maybe unfixable.

So she was somehow both unprepared and

unsurprised when Ellen knocked on her door one afternoon. The baby was napping and Katie was at Grandma's; the house was unnaturally quiet. Feeling the fatigue of early pregnancy, Jessie'd been contemplating a nap and wasn't happy to see a sleek, polished young woman on her doorstep. They were about the same age -- early thirties -- but the similarities ended there. The visitor's long black hair curled perfectly over her shoulders and her blue eyes were expertly made up to make them even brighter. She wore a simple sleeveless dress and towering stiletto heels. Jessie's eyes fell on her long, manicured nails wistfully; she could hardly remember having fingernails, let alone manicures. She had a sudden mental image of herself: hair that should have been washed this morning, but wasn't, now scraped back into a ponytail, T-shirt with drool on one shoulder, belly starting to pouch out already.

"Yes? May I help you?" she said.

The woman laughed easily. "I'm going to help you, honey."

"I don't want to buy anything," Jessie said quickly.

"Not selling anything but the truth. I'm here to talk to you about your husband."

"My husband?"

"You'd better let me come in," she said, "so we don't give the neighbors too much of a treat."

Numb with foreboding, Jessie stood aside and the woman stepped through the door in a cloud of expensive perfume.

She had a lot to say. Her name was Ellen McCowan, and she and Scott met when he bought his Porsche from her. She recited all the times they'd been together in his big new lakeside house and the romantic interludes in the boat -- neither of which Jessie had known existed. Of course, she knew about the Porsche because Scott drove it home. He wouldn't let the kids even sit inside it; he said their sticky hands would ruin the upholstery and they'd pee on the seats. Jessie realized her mind was wandering.

"I don't believe a word of this," she said unconvincingly. It was the first thing she'd said since Ellen started talking.

Ellen looked at her pityingly.

"Look, I can see you're in a tough spot here. I just thought you should be warned so you could protect yourself and your children. Scott has a lot of money now and you're entitled to at least half of it. You don't have to put up with his screwing around because you need his support. He's a cheap bastard except when it comes to himself. He wouldn't even advance me my rent money when I was short, and he never took me anyplace. Get a good lawyer, that's my advice."

"Please go," Jessie said and went to open the door and stand by it until Ellen had no choice but to leave. On the doorstep, she turned back.

"I'm sorry. You seem like a nice person. Good luck."

Jessie barely made it to the bathroom before she threw up in violent spasms. She pressed her burning forehead against the cool porcelain of the toilet and clasped her arms protectively around her belly, willing the baby inside to stay put. She had only a few minutes to lie still on the bathroom floor before she heard Daniel's calls. Nap time was over.

~*~

Jessie talked to her folks first. Her father was so angry he had to pace around in the backyard for a while. Her mother, looking stunned, sat at the kitchen table clutching a coffee cup.

"It's not that we're crazy about Scott," her mother said. "We always wondered what you saw in him. But, honey, it will be so hard on you, and we hate to think of the children growing up without their daddy."

"Well, to hell with him!" her father said, stomping back into the kitchen, slamming the door behind him explosively. "The kids are better off without a shit like him around. I never thought he was good enough for Jessie and now he's proved it. I'd like to shoot him right between those squinty eyes."

Eventually, her mother got up, poured out her cold coffee and put on a new pot. They blew their noses, took some deep breaths and settled down. There were plans to be made.

"I'll call Mick," her dad said.

Mick was Jessie's cousin and a lawyer.

"Dad, you always said Mick's a dirty street fighter," Jessie protested.

"That's exactly what you need right now."

Mick was delighted to represent her. He loved a fight, always had from the time they were kids. In their younger days, she'd carried bruises from many an encounter with Mick. Now he was just as enthusiastic about bruising Scott. He ferreted out information that she didn't see how he could possibly have gotten about Scott's investments and plans to divorce her.

"We'll serve him with divorce papers before he can serve you," Mick said happily. "Let's give the little turd a surprise."

He rehearsed her over and over for the scene they knew would be forthcoming. Jessie didn't think she could pull it off, but when Scott came roaring in the door, she saw him with new eyes. The sweet young college boy she'd loved was gone and she realized he'd been gone for a long time. Here was a man she didn't even like. For the first time, she didn't care what he thought or felt or how he reacted.

Star

I had an old high school friend, Sue, who became a realtor. I asked her to be on the lookout for a modest house that would be comfortable for a family of six and would also be a good investment for me.

"Wait. What now? A *modest* house?" she said. "Didn't I hear something about you winning the lottery? Why would you want a modest house?"

"It's not for us," I said. "I want a rental property."

"Oh, of course. Gotta put all that money someplace, right? The housing market's tight right now; give me a week."

At the end of the week, she called back.

"I'm not having a great deal of luck on your house search. There are a couple of properties you could look at, but they're in rough shape. I don't know how much time and money you want to spend on rehab. But I do have an idea. Why don't you make *your* house into a rental? You and Rowan will undoubtedly move to a bigger place sooner or later, maybe on the lake or in a gated community. You'll want something more in keeping with your new status. The house you live in now would be perfect for the family you've described. You've got three bedrooms on the main level and you could easily make another bedroom in the basement."

"Our house? But that's *ours*."

I thought of all the work we've done to make our middle-aged ranch house pretty and comfortable. It would be like leaving a family member to move now.

But a place on the lake where our nieces and nephews could go swimming, and where Rowan and I could sit together and watch the sun set over the water -- that sounded tempting. Nothing grand; we're not grand people and never will be. But a spacious house with plenty of bedrooms and bathrooms and maybe even a little guest house where our friends and relatives could come for a break -- that might be fun. And knowing that Jane and the kids would be living in our old house would make it easier to leave. It would still be cared for and loved.

"I need to talk it over with Rowan," I said, "but I think I like the idea."

I knew Scott had purchased a home on the lake, so I called and asked if I could drop by to see it. He sounded less than thrilled, but that's just Scott and I didn't take his tone personally. He was home that afternoon, so I took him up on his half-hearted invitation and drove out to his new place. I was surprised at how palatial it was. With all those little ones, I would have expected something more kid-friendly.

After we exchanged greetings and made a few minutes of small talk, I asked Scott how Jessie and the kids were adjusting to the new home. He looked uncomfortable.

"Uh, well, actually, they don't live here. Jessie and I are calling it quits," he said reluctantly.

I stared at him in astonishment. "Quits? You've got a baby on the way."

"Yeah. Jessie wants it this way," he said. He didn't meet my eyes.

I decided to let it drop. Not my business, but I was sure that Jessie hadn't suddenly chosen to have a baby and then raise three little ones on her own, no matter how much money she might get. Scott was a creep, but like I said, not my business.

He gave me the grand tour of the immaculately appointed house and grounds, ending at the boat dock where a sleek white speedboat bobbed up and down in the waves. Its name was painted on the side in fancy black cursive: Lucky Duck. True, that!

It was an impressive place but totally lacking in personal touches. Actually, it looked like someone else's house and Scott was just visiting. But he was full of homeowner's pride as he pointed out the view, the little man-made sandy beach, the infinity pool, elaborate pool house and outdoor sitting area complete with a huge stone fireplace. I made all the right "wow" noises. No point in raining on his parade.

"Very impressive," I said, as we settled on comfortable deck chairs by the pier. "Do you like living here? Would you recommend it?"

"Yeah, sure, I've got to live somewhere. I might move out of state, maybe to Hawaii or, I don't know, France."

He sounded pretentious and uncertain at the same time. I bit my tongue to ask how often he thought he'd see his kids if he lived in Hawaii. Not my business, not my business!

~*~

Sue was a lot more enthusiastic about searching for big houses for us. She had Rowan and me out looking the very next day. We didn't have a rigid mental list of must-haves, so we were easy to please. A lot of her yak about granite counter tops, stainless steel appliances and open concepts whistled right over our heads. There was one house, though, that we both liked at once. It was a rustic log structure with a wall of windows facing the lake. Six big bedrooms, each with its own bathroom, a huge, eat-in kitchen, and best of all, a wrap-around screened porch. One feature made Rowan's eyes shine: a winding staircase banister made of tree branches. It was so "him" that it made us both laugh.

The house was vacant, the owner having been transferred out of state. Sue confided that he was making double mortgage payments and was "motivated to sell," as they say in real-estatese. There was a little bargaining, but not too much. We could afford to pay a fair price and it sounded like the seller needed a break. We brought a cashier's check for the full amount to the closing. I don't think the meaning of the money sunk in for either Rowan or me until then.

I phoned Jane with the news that her "new" house would be ready for move-in in a couple of weeks and until that time, I would continue paying for her and the kids to remain at the motel. She was excited and grateful, but she also had questions I hadn't considered: is the house on a bus line? Are the public schools within walking distance and are they good ones? Were there any other renters in the vicinity, or would she and her family "break the block," causing neighborly resentment? Jane was proving to be more savvy than my first impression of her as a beaten-down, impoverished mother suggested.

Rowan and I drove over and picked up Jane and her family the following Saturday so they could have a look at what would be their home. The kids' eyes were wide as Jane introduced them to us.

"This is Julia, my oldest, she's ten; the twins are Jacob and Jonas, and they're eight; Jennifer is four and our baby, Joy, is two."

Rowan laughed. "Jumpin' Jiminy! All J's?"

Jane smiled back. "Their Daddy's name is James, and I'm Jane, and we thought it would be cute. Seemed like a good idea at the time."

Her voice trailed off and her face clouded over. I knew Jane and her husband were separated -- that he had actually abandoned the family during hard times -- and old memories had to be harrowing for her. I changed the subject.

"Come on, everybody; let's take a look at your new house."

I was touched to see how enthusiastically Rowan entered into the kids' excitement as they explored their home. We'd wanted kids when we first got married and then the years passed without them and we settled into childlessness. I'd long ago put parenthood out of my mind, but it looked like Rowan hadn't. I felt a lump in my throat as I watched him carrying baby Joy tenderly from room to room. Jane was watching, too.

"You have a good man, Star," she said. "He'd make a good daddy."

None of us knew how prophetic her words were.

CHAPTER NINE

Marilyn

I spotted a church marquee one day when I was running errands: "Join First Methodist's Singles-Over-Sixty Group," it said. Well, why not? I'd been looking for a way to meet men and what could be safer than a church? There was a meeting that very evening and impulsively I decided to go. I wasn't a member of First Methodist so I could be pretty sure that no one I knew would be there to see if I turned out to be a miserable failure among the Over-Sixties.

I spent the rest of the day shopping for a new outfit and getting my hair and nails done at the priciest salon in town -- a door I'd never dared to darken pre-lottery. At the appointed time, I turned up at the church feeling like an unfamiliar version of myself. I found the Ladies Room first and did some superfluous primping, just for the fun of looking at myself in the mirror.

Despite the best efforts of an unnamed and unsung decorating committee, the church hall looked and smelled like every other church hall I'd ever visited: leftover hints of coffee, candle-wax and institutional cleaner in the air, green vinyl tile waxed to a high gloss on the floor, and bland beige concrete block walls with a few highly-colored depictions of an Anglo-Saxon Jesus on display. I wondered about the set-up: a couple of dozen small tables with a single flower in a bud vase in the center and two chairs each. Some of the chairs were already occupied by ladies dressed to the nines, coiffed, scented and clearly as nervous as I was.

It turned out that the Over-Sixties were having a speed dating night. I'd heard of it, seen something about it on television, but never had I expected to participate. However, there I was. In for a penny, in for a pound, as Mom used to say.

We were welcomed by a woman in a sensible navy pantsuit, sequined eye glasses and a wispy white hairdo. She stepped up to the microphone like an old pro.

"Ladies and gentlemen, if I may have your attention, please."

Throats cleared, clothing rustled and chairs scraped as we all settled down. I sat at the nearest empty table. Our mistress of ceremonies continued.

"Most of you have been to Speed Dating Night before, but for you newcomers, here's how it works. The ladies sit at the tables and the gentlemen circulate. The bell rings at five-minute intervals and the gentlemen move on to the next table. If you want to get better acquainted, you may exchange phone numbers or agree to meet at the social hour afterwards. If not, no explanations are necessary. Please join me now in prayer."

Heads quickly ducked and eyes closed obediently all over the room.

"Heavenly Father, we ask your blessing on our fellowship tonight. Let all we do reflect your honor and glory. Amen." In exactly the same tone, she added, "Now! Let's mingle!"

The lights dimmed and we were off.

The first man drifted to my table on a zephyr of cologne. He was about my age, despite efforts to the contrary. Razor-cut hair was sprayed into immobility and his designer jeans were worn low to accommodate a bit of belly. He had a smile too full of unnaturally white teeth. Perched on the edge of the chair, he told me outright that he was looking for a younger woman.

"Or at least someone who looks younger," he added graciously.

That pretty much killed any chance of further conversation and it was with great relief on both our parts that we heard the bell ring.

He moved away, to be replaced by a smallish, balding fellow who looked closer to forty than sixty. Levis and shirttails accentuated his boyish appearance.

"How old are you, again?" I asked.

"Actually, I'm not sixty," he confessed. "Not even close. The singles crowd my own age scares me to death, so I thought I'd come to this one just for practice. I sort of forgot that you'd all be so...."

"Old?" I said.

"Well, yes."

He smiled, and for the first time, I saw that he was attractive in a nerdish way. "I'm sorry, I'm wasting your time," he said.

"Not at all," I said, smiling back. "I'm just here

for the flattery and the free refreshments."

We were laughing when the bell rang. My next visitor approached haltingly on a walker. He declined to take a seat, saying it was too hard to get back up again. Hanging between the handles of his walker, he assessed me silently.

"Do you have any nursing experience?" he finally asked.

"Nursing? Well, I took care of my mother for a lot of years, but I'm not a nurse."

"Got your own car? Able to drive at night, are you?"

"Uh, well, yeah." I couldn't imagine where all this was heading.

"Daytimes free?"

"Why are you asking?"

"Need somebody to get me to my doctor appointments and do a few things around the house. And sometimes I like to go out at night. I'll pay, of course. See, my health isn't what it used to be…"

He launched into an organ recital that took us right up to the bell, the blessed, merciful bell. Then he shuffled off to the next table. I heard him say, when he arrived, "Got any nursing experience?"

The next man told me in great detail about his success in the dry-cleaning business. The one after that was a recent widower, recent enough to tear up as he described what a wonderful person his late wife was. He was followed by a sports fan who lost interest in me when I confessed I didn't have a favorite football team. Then came the guy whose conversation consisted of an angry recitation of current events that proved we were living in the

Last Days. He at least didn't need or expect a response; "uh huh" was plenty for him.

When the lady in the pantsuit again took the mike to announce that the speed dating part of the evening was over and we were now welcome to have refreshments and continue our conversations, I picked up my purse and made a quick exit. Okay, so the Over-Sixties didn't pan out. The evening had at least provided me with a new appreciation of my own company. I headed for home.

Later, snuggled into my oldest pajamas, sipping a fragrant cup of Darjeeling, I gave myself a little pep talk. *There has to be a place for me. Forget about meeting men; I just need to feel that I'm a member of the community again.*

I Googled volunteer opportunities on my laptop. (What *can't* you Google?) After sifting through a list of service organizations that needed help, I e-mailed my willingness to serve meals at a homeless shelter downtown on Tuesday afternoons between four and 8 p.m.

That's where I met Sam.

Darren

Mom and I had another talk about moving. She was adamantly against it.

"This has been my home for forty years," she said. "This is where your father and I raised you, it's where Dad spent his last days, right there in that recliner, and it's where I intend to live until I die."

"Okay, okay, but how about sprucing up the place a little? You've always said you wished we had a guest bath and a coat closet. What about adding onto the front of the house, putting in a proper foyer, maybe blowing up the attic to make a second-floor master suite?"

"For you, Darren? I'll stay in the bedroom I shared with your Dad. Do you want a second floor master suite?"

"Well, no, I guess not. Actually, Mom, I'm thinking about moving out."

"I *knew* it! I knew you'd get around to that eventually, now that you're a rich man. This old place isn't good enough for you now, is it?"

"C'mon, Mom. I'm thirty-four years old. When you were thirty-four, you had a husband, a home and a little boy -- me. Do you want me to go through life never having those things?"

That got to her. She took off her glasses and polished them on the hem of her blouse while she thought for a moment. When she spoke, her voice was soft.

"Of course not, son. I want you to have it all. I just get scared at the thought of living alone for the first time in my life. You know, I went from my father's house to my husband's house, and I've never had the experience of being on my own before."

Her eyes looked huge behind her clean bifocals and I noticed they were full of tears. I felt a stab of empathy and tried not to let it make me weak.

"But isn't it kind of liberating?" I said. "Wouldn't you like to do just as you please without considering anyone else? You can travel if you want to, or hire a maid and a cook. Join a gym and work out in spandex."

She was smiling now. Mom's smiles are rare but they are beautiful. I caught a glimpse of the young girl my father married. I gave her a hug, although we are not, as a rule, a hugging family. To my surprise, she hugged me back, hard.

"Darren, you go on. If it means moving, or traveling, or getting married to that Bella girl, or whatever - you do it. I may not like it and I may act ugly, but ignore me for once in your life. Don't waste any more precious time drinking vodka in your room after you think I'm asleep."

Yep, that's my Mom. You can't put anything over on her and she'll zing you when you least expect it. I knew from long experience that this benevolent mood wouldn't last, but I decided to take her at her word. I couldn't afford to pass up any chance, however tenuous, for a happy ending.

Marilyn

She was huddled in the corner of the building that housed the homeless shelter, making herself as small as she could. Head down, ears back, teeth bared in what was clearly meant to be a smile, her whole demeanor said, "I mean no harm. I could use a friend."

We never had a dog, Mom and I. Mom maintained that I was allergic, but either I outgrew it or my so-called allergy was just an excuse to keep me from bugging her, because, as a child, my fondest wish was for a puppy. It was one of those things I'd given up as impractical when I got older.

I looked at this dog and she looked back at me, eyes shining, ears flattened, tail wagging. She was medium sized, the same yellowish-buff color as a coyote, with a white mask on her face. It's easy to read more into a dog's face than is truly there, but to me, she seemed to be pleading for help. When I held out my hand, she inched forward and I saw that her belly almost dragged the ground.

"Oh! You're pregnant," I said aloud.

She wagged her tail harder at the sound of my voice and kept coming slowly toward my outstretched hand. She gave it one lick, then lowered her head, turned around and got back into her corner.

"Not only pregnant, but about to have those puppies, I think. Don't go anywhere while I get some help."

I went into the shelter and asked to speak to whoever was in charge. A harried woman emerged from a door that opened into the kitchen. She wore a white, food-stained apron, a hairnet and plastic gloves.

"Yes, may I help you?" she asked.

"There's a dog outside on the street. She looks like she's about to have puppies and I wondered if someone here could help her."

The woman looked at me in disbelief.

"This is a homeless shelter," she said slowly, enunciating clearly to be sure I understood. "We look after *people*. Right now, I have a dining room full of hungry *people.* Did you come to help serve the meal?"

"Well, yes, but the dog--" I broke off, clearly

having lost my audience.

She turned back toward the kitchen, speaking over her shoulder. "If you want to volunteer, we can get you started right away, but I'm afraid we don't have time for dogs. After everyone has been served, I'll call the pound and ask them to come and get her. Best I can do right now."

I went back outside and the dog was still there, now curled up in a tight ball, licking frantically at her hind quarters. Somehow -- don't ask me how -- I knew that meant birth was imminent. I couldn't just leave her there on the city street with no shelter and no care. I retrieved my car from the parking lot, pulled up at the curb beside the dog, hefted her up somehow and put her on the back seat. She made no sound of protest or pain, going limp in my arms. We went home.

It was a long night. The pallet of old towels on the floor was soaked with blood and fluids as puppy after puppy emerged. The mother dog cleaned them efficiently, bit the umbilical cord in two and tucked them close to her, where they nosed around for breakfast. Finally, as the sky began to lighten, it was over. Four puppies were alive and well, looking like scrawny little rats as they nursed. Of course, I had no dog food, so I served the mother scrambled eggs and toast. She ate hungrily and then drank an enormous amount of water. Finally she lay her head down on her paws and slept, oblivious to the tiny balls of fur beside her.

I surveyed the little family through eyes burning with sleeplessness. What in the world was I going to do with five dogs?

Scott

So now I had a divorce to get through before I could really enjoy my new life. There were frequent meetings with Lawrence, plotting strategy. I was disappointed with his lack of killer instincts, though.

"Lawrence, come *on*, grow a pair, will you?" I snapped at him during one session.

"I'm not going to give Jessie half. I'll support the kids, I'll educate them when it's time, but damned if she's going to live in luxury on my money."

"What you don't seem to realize," Lawrence said, "is that Jessie holds all the cards. This is an equitable division state. That means assets are to be divided, and not necessarily 50/50. You've been married ten years; Jessie is pregnant with your third child. A sympathetic jury might give her more than half of your money. Your only prerogative is to decide how difficult you want to make your life in the meantime."

Odd, how he echoed Jessie's words.

"There are plenty of other lawyers around here, if you don't have the stomach for a fight."

Lawrence looked at me wearily. "There isn't going to be a fight, Scott. Go before any judge, go before any jury with one woman on the panel, and Jessie will get her half and maybe more."

I fumed about it for a few days, and then I decided that nine million was still a lot of money and if meeting Jessie's demands was the price of freedom, then I'd buy it. Giving her the money scorched me to my soul, but I finally signed the agreement. It called for me to have the kids every third weekend, but what the hell was I going to do with two little kids? I figured I'd stop in and see them at home.

The first of my "Daddy" weekends came and I buzzed by the house at about ten on Saturday morning, planning to run around in the yard with the kids for an hour or so and then be on my way. Jessie had two little suitcases packed and waiting by the door.

"Here's Daddy," she said, when I entered the house without knocking. "Here's Daddy, come to take you to his new house for the night."

Katie came running to hug my knees and Daniel called, "Da da da da," from his highchair, banging on the tray with his spoon. Gotta admit, it was good to see the little buggers again.

"Hey, I can't take them for the night," I said. "I don't have beds or cribs or whatever, and there's no kid food, and -- well, I'm not ready."

"The agreement says your custody weekend starts today. You knew that. You've got nothing but time so if you're not ready, that's a choice you made."

"You want *your* kids to come to a house that isn't child-proofed, to sleep god knows where, to play next to an unfenced pool and a lake?"

Jessie wavered. I knew she would.

"Okay, Scott, you win this round. I don't want *our* kids in danger. But when your next custodial weekend comes, I expect you to be ready. Don't make me go back to the judge. Do whatever you have to do -- hire a nanny, fence in part of your yard, fix up two bedrooms for them -- whatever it takes to make them safe at your house. And I'll be coming over to check."

All doable suggestions, although I hadn't thought of any of them. I promised Her Bossiness that I'd follow her instructions to the letter, if she'd just let me off the hook for today. When she agreed, I took the kids out into the back yard as I'd planned, pushed them on the swings, rolled the ball for Katie to kick, built sand castles with Daniel, ran them through the sprinkler, and delivered them back to their mother wet, sandy and cranky, within an hour.

I was done with childcare chores for the weekend and the remaining time stretched invitingly before me. Now that I was no longer working, there wasn't much difference between weekdays and weekends, but there was still a psychological kick to Saturday and Sunday. The sun shone, the boat bobbed gently at the pier and the swimming pool sparkled. I wished I had someone to impress. I decided to hit the bar scene that night and see who was out there.

Turns out, there are plenty of women out there and like the song says, they all get better-looking at closing time. I wandered from bar to bar, checking out the talent in each one. I bought round after round of drinks, but the beautiful women were definitely not interested in me and they let me know it in a hundred ego-deflating ways. The ones who smiled back were mediocre at best, but as the evening progressed I knew I'd be settling for one of them.

The girl who agreed to come home with me

seemed nice enough but not too bright. She left her girlfriends with a triumphant smile. I guess she was the winner of whatever competition they had going. She was flatteringly impressed with my car and my house and that made me feel like a big man. But we quickly ran out of conversation and the trip to bed reeked of desperation. I don't even remember her name. Surely I knew it at the time.

Picking up a woman for a one-night stand was a first for me, and after I dropped her off at her apartment the next morning, I began to worry that I'd caught some awful disease from her. A girl who lets herself be picked up in a bar -- who knows what she might be carrying? That's one concern a married man doesn't usually have. I made myself a note to call my doctor for a check-up on Monday.

The rest of Sunday was spent sleeping off a mild but unpleasant hangover. I didn't hear another human voice all day and by four o'clock I thought the sun would never set. As weekends go, it wasn't that great. I told myself I needed to find a better class of women.

There was one I had my eye on. You wouldn't have to worry about catching a venereal disease from her. She worked in Larry Bickler's office, at the front desk so she was the first person you saw when you came in. I'd talk to her for a few minutes if I had to wait for Larry. Her name was Kylie, but I was willing to overlook that. None of us can help what our parents name us.

Anyway, Kylie was a little younger than me. She was pretty in a soft kind of way and there was a picture on her desk of her with a smiling toddler that she said was her little girl. But there was no husband; I asked, but she didn't provide any details. I made some moves on Kylie but she didn't seem to notice. She treated me with the same friendly courtesy she showed everyone else. I wanted her to notice me, treat me special. You'd think she'd pay attention to one of the firm's most important clients.

One day I just point-blank asked her out. She smiled that same friendly smile and said she didn't date clients. I persisted, repeating the invitation every time I went into the office. She kept smiling and saying no thank you. I even mentioned it to Larry, thinking maybe he could influence her.

"Oh, I doubt Kylie would go out with you," he said, emphasizing "you," which really pissed me off. "She doesn't date much."

"I suppose you're saving her for yourself," I said sourly.

Larry gave me a funny look and changed the subject. One day there was no one else in the reception area and I took the opportunity to press my case with Kylie.

"Come on, just dinner, or not even dinner -- drinks. I'll pay for your baby-sitter, how's that?"

Kylie smiled impersonally. "I hate to keep repeating myself, Scott, but no thank you."

"Just tell me why not," I said. I was getting mad.

Kylie lost her smile. "Okay, I guess you won't take no for an answer until I do. I won't go out with you because you dumped your wife as soon as you came into money, leaving her pregnant and with two little kids. I won't go out with you because you have a reputation as a player, and I don't intend to be played. I won't go out with you because you think your money can get you anything you want. And finally, I won't go out with you because I have a little girl who can't wait until I get home so she can spend time with her mommy. So, again: thanks but no thanks, and please don't ask me again."

"Don't worry, I won't."

From then on, I treated her like the hired help she was. But it rankled. Kylie seemed like a class act. Didn't I rate a classy woman? I tried not to examine that question too closely.

~*~

Life settled down. The excitement of the lottery win receded into the background. You can get used to anything, even money. Unstructured days stretched before me. I actually offered to keep the kids more often than my scheduled weekends, but Jessie said no.

"I don't want their days disrupted," she said. "They need to have the security of routine as they adjust to their dad being gone from their everyday lives. And soon they'll have to get used to a new sibling."

So I puttered around the house, took the boat out, watched some T.V., drank too much beer. I never was a reader and had no hobbies. Volunteering was for suckers, I always thought - why work for nothing? And I sure as hell wasn't getting another job.

What do rich people do? I asked myself. Well,

they travel, I figured, so I tried a short cruise to the Bahamas. There was an outbreak of norovirus on the ship, wouldn't you know, and I spent the five days in my cabin alternately sitting on or whirling to embrace the toilet.

What else do the rich do? Buy things. Okay. I already had a house, boat and car, so now I hired a decorator and allowed her to go on a marathon spending spree to furnish the house in grand style. After that, everything was so fancy that I didn't feel at home in my own home, but it looked great.

I noticed that rich people also went to charity functions, so I got myself invited to a few, only to realize that there were some very pricey strings attached to those invites. Hey, if I'd wanted to give my money away, I could have joined that cockamamie scholarship foundation that the others set up.

Finally, I fell into a numbing routine. I'd sleep in because I'd been up drinking until late. Then I'd sit in the sun until the worst of my hangover lifted. If it was a nice day, I'd take the boat out and tool around the lake awhile. Rainy days meant old movies on television. I was strict with myself about not drinking before five o'clock but more and more often I found myself watching the hands creep around to that magic number when I could once again court oblivion.

I hated to admit it even to myself, but I was bored and depressed. Money didn't seem to keep the black dog away from my door. The weekends that I had the kids were a relief; at least I had something to do.

When the new baby was born, Jessie named him Morris, after her dad. Did she consult me? No, she did not. In fact, she didn't even tell me he was here until he was a week old. I went to the house with two dozen supermarket roses but her mother said Jessie was sleeping, tipped the flowers into the trash bin and shut the door firmly in my face.

CHAPTER TEN

Bella

The lights were bright in Nashville, just as innumerable country songs said they would be. At 4:30 on a Monday afternoon, I stood on the sidewalk in front of the Bluebird Café. In a line of wannabe cowgirls in boots and fringe, I wore skinny jeans and a white tee shirt that fit like second skin -- I was going for anti-glitz. We were all waiting to sign up for open mike night and a more nervous, twitchy bunch you'd have to look hard to find. I finally reached the front of the line only to hear that registration had closed for the day.

"Come on back next week," said the young man with the clipboard and the heartbreaking smile, handing me a "Play Next Time" ticket. "We'll put your name at the top of the list."

It had taken just about my entire reserve of courage to get that far, but there wasn't a thing I could do about it. Except wait. I vowed I'd put that extra week to good use.

So I worshiped at the shrine of the old Ryman Auditorium, hearing in its silence the echoes of all the singers who'd performed there. I thought of

Dolly, with her coat of many colors, and how Loretta had driven around the South with her husband, peddling her demo tapes to remote radio stations. I thought of Hank, so lonesome he could cry, his short life ending in the back seat of a Cadillac. And Faith, adopted as an infant to a Mississippi family, growing up singing for prisoners in the local lock-up, at church, at 4-H luncheons, – anywhere they'd let a talented little girl sing. They and so many others came to Nashville and they made it. Maybe, maybe, maybe I could make it, too.

I haunted the shops, putting together outfit after outfit, experimenting with dancehall girl, country-rock punk, sweetheart of the rodeo. I'd stick with anti-glitz, I finally decided, and my trademark look would be jeans, boots and fitted white tee shirts.

I hung around performance venues, listening to the artists who were drawing crowds. My shyness prevented me from approaching the stars, but I got acquainted with some real professionals, the back-up musicians. They were the strong spine of Nashville, lending their talents to both live performances and recordings, shifting and reconfiguring into ad hoc groups to supply whatever was needed. One of them was a picker named Boyd Ackerly, a bona fide Texas cowboy. He'd come to Nashville hoping to make it as a single act, but soon found out he didn't have that kind of drive.

"I like playing in a band," he said, "and I like getting a regular paycheck and I like backing up singers." Only he said "sangers."

That was perfect for me, because truth to tell,

my picking skills left a lot to be desired. My guitar was more of a fashion accessory; it was all I could do to strum a few basic chords that I'd learned from friends who played. The Bluebird didn't allow backing tapes but did allow a singer to bring one or two musicians as accompanists. Luckily, I could afford to hire Boyd. He'd proven to be a font of inside information and didn't hesitate to give me tips for crafting my stage persona.

"Lower necklines, sweetheart," he said, "higher boot heels, tighter jeans. Get your hair cut at Norma's. Have a session with this gal," handing me a business card for a vocal coach, "and get your stage makeup done. You don't want to look like nobody else right from the start, so people know you the minute you walk onstage and remember you afterwards."

Nashville was full of beautiful young people. Everywhere I turned, there were girls who looked like they were stars already. I knew if I was going to stand out, I needed a trademark. Sexy simplicity wasn't as easy to achieve as it sounded, but I followed all of Boyd's advice.

And we practiced, lord, how we practiced. Boyd said we needed to prepare more than one song, just in case.

"Won't hurt to be ready," he said. "We'll probably need it sooner or later, anyway."

"I'll be lucky to get through one song in front of that crowd. What if I screw this up, Boyd? What if the audience hates me? Or almost worse than that: what if they clap politely for a few seconds?"

"Yeah, what if that happens? Will you die? Or

will you maybe learn something you need to know to improve your performance? You better forget the what if's and believe in yourself, because if you don't, sure as hell nobody else will."

Over and over those two songs we went, until I felt I could sing them perfectly if somebody jabbed me awake with a pin in the middle of the night. I still wasn't very good on my guitar but I felt more confident strumming a few chords as I sang, while Boyd's back-up made me sound polished. If only he could have made me *feel* polished.

"Not sure I can do this," I wailed late one night. We'd been rehearsing all day and I was exhausted. "Pretty sure I *can't* do this."

"Pretty sure you *can*," Boyd said. "Pretty sure you dang well will."

Sometimes all it takes is one person who believes you can do it, somebody who knows the ropes, whose opinion you respect. Somebody who will give you a kick right in the seat of the pants when you need it. Despite my nerves, I trusted Boyd, at least enough to keep on trying.

Now I was standing on the familiar sidewalk outside the Bluebird Café again, this time under an umbrella, worrying that the drizzle would make my hair frizzy, worrying about getting my new thousand dollar boots wet, worrying about -- *Oh, my God!* -- performing before a crowd of country music fans. Nashville fans. Any confidence I'd gained from singing my own songs at little bars back home disappeared like ink on wet paper.

The young man signed me up this time, bestowing his smile like a blessing, and I took my place in the audience to wait my turn. The Bluebird Cafe isn't a large venue; it seats about 90 people but they are there to listen. Established artists, agents scouting for the next big thing -- you never know who'll be there. I recognized several famous faces. That didn't help my nerves.

The singers/songwriters who went before me were experienced, professional and poised. *They* accompanied themselves expertly on their guitars. *They* smiled confidently at the audience. *They* hadn't made twenty trips to the bathroom that day, I'd bet.

I slumped further and further down in my seat, wishing hard that I'd taken Darren up on his offer to come with me to Nashville. But I'd thought I'd be less nervous if no one I knew was listening. Now I'd give my new boots for a friendly face. I tried to ignore the ominous rumbling in my gut.

The crowd was quiet and intent during performances, then generous with applause. Their respect for those who dared to get up on stage came from an understanding of how hard it was. I was shivering with fear when I heard my name called.

Somehow I made my way to the front. Going up the three steps to the little stage, I caught the pointy toe of my boot and pitched forward. I heard the collective "Oooooh," behind me. There was a smattering of applause when I managed to catch myself before falling flat on my face. A voice said, "Don't let it throw you, honey, you can do it." That got me up those steps and onto the stage.

I turned to them, a faceless mass rustling and whispering somewhere beyond the bright stage lights. For an endless moment, I just stood there, my voice caught in my throat. The rustling and whispering grew louder. I heard isolated comments: *"She's scared to death. Sometimes they just freeze like that. She can't do it, bless her heart."*

It was the "bless her heart" that gave me a shove. In the South, you can say anything about anybody if you end with "bless her heart." What it really means is "what a loser!" I got a grip.

Pretend nobody's out there, Boyd had said, sing like you're home alone, sing like you don't care. I gave myself a mental shake and glanced at him; he nodded and winked. *Just let me not throw up in front of everyone. Just let me live through this.*

I guess I sang. I must have, because the audience was making noise. I couldn't see them but I heard them, the sound breaking over me like a wave. It seemed to go on forever while I stood there blinking and smiling. I realized the emcee was talking to me.

"Have you got anything else?" he asked. "They want another one."

"Oh. Yes. Sure."

Thank God we'd rehearsed two songs. Boyd grinned at me and struck the opening chords. The audience quieted, and into that quiet I poured out everything I had in me. Every hope and fear, dream and triumph, every heartache. I was outside myself, watching a dark-haired girl with a useless guitar hanging from her neck, belting out her song straight from the gut. When I sang the last note, my new Nashville friends, all ninety of them, were on their feet, yelling, whistling, stomping their boots on the floor. How we loved each other, that audience and I!

A current of electricity passed between us, lighting me up. In that instant, shyness was forgotten and applause became my drug of choice. I wanted more.

Darren

I was in the audience at the Bluebird Café when Bella took the place by storm. Slouched down in the very last row behind a big-haired lady, I made sure she didn't see me. She'd made it clear she wanted to tackle her Nashville debut alone. But I couldn't stay away. My heart stopped when she tripped going up on the stage, and I broke into a sweat when she paused for what seemed like eternity before launching into her number. I think I must have felt what fathers experience when their children perform. Only my feelings for Bella were anything but paternal.

God, I was so proud of her! When the crowd leaped to its feet and cheered the roof down, I felt tears running down my face. I slipped out while she was taking her bows, before the house lights came up. Couldn't risk her seeing me. I was standing on the sidewalk trying to compose myself when I felt a tap on my shoulder and there she was. Her hands were shaking and her eyes were enormous.

"Darren, did you see? Did you see?" she demanded.

"I did, Bella. You were terrific. They loved you. I'm sorry, I know you told me to stay home, but I just couldn't."

"It doesn't matter, I'm so glad you're here. I'm glad you were out there in the audience, so you can tell me what it was like."

We walked to an all-night diner, found a booth in the corner and ordered coffee. Bella pelted me with questions: how did she look up there, did she look scared, what did the people around me say about her performance, could I understand the lyrics? I wouldn't have burst her bubble of pride and accomplishment even if it meant making up fiction on the spot, but it wasn't necessary. The truth was good enough.

Finally she ran down, yawned enormously and let her shoulders droop.

"Time you get to bed," I said.

She raised her head and looked straight into my eyes. "I don't want you to go," she said. "Stay with me tonight, Darren."

Part of me jumped at the chance to be Bella's lover; after all, wasn't that what I'd been craving? But I didn't want to take advantage of the heat her moment of triumph had generated. What if she woke the next morning and thought, *what have I done?* I didn't think I could stand to be one of Bella's regrets. Overwhelmed by the scent of her hair, by her eyes so dark they looked black, by my desire for her, somehow I still knew I wanted to be in it for the long haul, not a one-night stand. I hesitated, and cursed myself for hesitating.

"Let me walk you back to your hotel," I finally said.

We walked the churning Nashville streets in silence, hand in hand. We entered her hotel lobby and rode the elevator to her floor without a word. At her door, she swiped the key card and pushed open the door without letting go of my hand. She gave it a tug and we were inside.

"Bella, I don't want you to regret..." I began.

But then Bella put her arms around me and rational thought left the building. Our first kiss was both awkward and all-engulfing.

"Are you sure this is what you want right now?" I murmured into her hair.

"Darren. Shut up."

So I did, and all my dreams and desires melted into reality. Making love to Bella simply sealed her in my heart. What it meant to her, I couldn't tell. She was always hard to read and physical intimacy didn't bring any big lightning bolt of clarity. But it changed things. We were different with each other after that night -- more at ease, more attuned. I longed to be sure of her love, to buy a huge diamond engagement ring, to have a big white wedding with our family and friends around us, but I instinctively knew to steer clear of any talk of commitment. Whatever she could give me would have to be enough.

Marilyn

I named the mama dog Samantha, but she quickly became Sam. She looked like a Sam, a bit world-weary -- like she rolled her own cigarettes -- like she'd been around the block a few times. I guess she had. I don't know what kind of dog Sam was. All kinds, I suppose. Her best feature was her smile. I recognized it as a smile and not a snarl the first time I saw it. Maybe it was the way one ear stood up and one flopped down, or her soulful amber eyes, but somehow you just knew this was a dog who would never bite you. I loved her. When I talked to her, she would leave the puppies and come to lean against my knees, gazing up at me seriously. It made a nice change from talking to myself.

The puppies were an evenly divided set of males and females. I named them, too: Jack and Jill, Donny and Marie. I know, not imaginative.

If you want to have a good day, live it with a bunch of puppies. They played; they yipped, they peed on the floor; they wrestled and ate and fell into sudden deep slumbers. It was endlessly entertaining. I didn't spend any more time thinking about being lonely or living alone -- because I wasn't.

Looking back, I realize that it never even occurred to me that Sam might belong to someone. And if it had, I would have thought that owner didn't deserve her, letting her wander around the city streets neglected and pregnant.

I gave Sam a couple weeks to recover from giving birth and then I looked in the Yellow Pages for a nearby vet. Time for a check-up. I made an appointment with a Dr. James Miller and on the appointed day, loaded up Sam and the puppies. Dr. Miller turned out to be about my age and had friendly laugh crinkles at the corners of his eyes. As he examined Sam, I told him how I'd come upon her and about the night her pups were born.

"I don't think she belongs to anybody," I said.

"Let's just scan for a microchip," Dr. Miller said, running the scanner over Sam's back. "Nope, she doesn't have one. Judging from the prominence of her ribs, she's missed some meals. I'd say she's a stray. Or should I say was?"

That settled it. Sam was my dog now. I went home and researched the internet to find the most nutritious brand of dog food and then bought big bags of it, a bright red collar and leash and ceramic bowls for food and water. I paid extra to have her name painted on them.

When the puppies got older and could do without her for a while, we started going for daily walks, Sam and me. I'd bundle the pups into a big cardboard box to await our return in relative safety, snap on Sam's leash and off we'd go. Walking a dog was new to me, but she was an easy companion. No unruly pulling on the leash like some of the dogs we saw. Every day we ventured a little farther, finally settling on a circuit of the neighborhood and park that took about an hour. We seldom missed a day. I noticed my clothes were becoming looser.

When the puppies were four weeks old, I took them in for check-ups, followed by more appointments for their puppy shots at six, nine, twelve and sixteen weeks. I saw more of Dr. Miller than anyone else. He was starting to feel like a friend and I listened when he said Sam should be spayed so she wouldn't have any more litters.

"We'll spay and neuter the pups, too, when they're old enough. There are already too many dogs in shelters," he said, "not that your dogs would ever end up in a shelter."

My dogs? Plural? I hadn't thought about what to do with the puppies when they stopped being adorable babies and turned into a pack of four -- no, with Sam, five adult dogs. Looking at them tumbling around, biting each other's ears, chewing each other's paws, I wondered if they even knew where one stopped and the other began. It made me feel sad to think of them going off alone to new homes, leaving the security of siblings and mother. Then I thought, well, why do they have to? It's not like I can't afford to keep them all.

It meant more visits to the vet -- so many that Dr. Miller asked me to call him Jim. I felt shy about that, so I compromised by calling him Dr. Jim, like his staff did. I found him immensely sympathetic and easy to talk to, and the story of my lottery win came out naturally in the conversation one day.

"Now I feel better about your vet bills," he said, and that was all. Knowing about the money didn't make him treat me any differently.

The babies needed all their inoculations before they could safely face the world, but the day finally came when Dr. Jim said they could go along with Sam and me on our walks. I bought four more red collars and leashes, harnessed them all up and set off a meandering, tangled-up, hilarious walk. We drew a good deal of attention, especially from small children, and when we got back home I reflected that I'd talked to more people during that walk than I normally encountered in a week.

The pups loved to be outside, so I hired a contractor to build a dog-proof fence around my back yard. I bought a child's wading pool and put about six inches of water in it just for the joy of watching the fat little guys splash. Sam would sometimes lower herself into the water, too, with a look of dignified gratification on her face. Life was good until the day a knock at the door announced a visit from the city code enforcement officer.

"Miz Simmons?"

"It's Miss."

"Miz Simmons, I got a complaint here about the number of dogs at your house."

"I've been very careful not to let them bother any of my neighbors. I don't know what anyone would have to complain about."

"Yes, ma'am, but the fact is, the city ordinance don't allow for more'n four dogs at a resy-dence. How many you got?"

"Five."

"Well, I'm sure sorry, but that's one too many. You reckon you could find another home for at least one of them?"

He handed me a notice that stated I had ten days to comply with zoning regulations or face a fine. Even knowing I could pay whatever fines the city wanted to levy didn't lessen my anxiety. In my family, we obeyed the law.

After he left, I called Dr. Jim in a panic.

"What am I going to do?" I wailed. "I can't get rid of any of them."

"Calm down, Marilyn. Remember, you are not without resources. Why don't you move? Why don't you get a place in the country where the city ordinances don't apply? Then you can have as many pets as you want."

It struck me as a totally impractical idea, but I thanked him politely. After we hung up, I gave his suggestion some thought. Why *not* move? What was keeping me here in this house now that Mother was gone? I knew Star and Rowan were moving, Scott had already bought a new house, and Bella was trying her luck in Nashville with Darren at her side.

That left me, still stuck in my same old rut. I made a decision right then to unstick myself.

CHAPTER ELEVEN

Bella

After that night in the Bluebird Café, my career took off like a rocket. A Nashville agent so famous that even I had heard of her, Suzi Lanier, was among the half dozen who contacted me the next day. She told me that Mary Jordan, a member of the hot new girl group, LadyBugs, had been in the audience for my performance. The LadyBugs were on the cusp of achieving country stardom after a big hit record. They had fans, and once you have a loyal fan base in country music, they stick with you forever.

"I wonder if you'd have time to drop by my office," Suzi said on the phone.

"Of course. But why... I mean, I'm flattered you'd even know who I am, but are you sure you've got the right person?"

Suzi had a deep laugh, right from her belly. "Yup, I'm sure. Come around three, okay?"

The intervening hours were spent imagining every possible scenario that might prompt Suzi Lanier to contact *me*. I was so nervous I asked Darren to go with me for moral support. We walked the block twice looking for the right building, and by the time we found it, I felt sweat trickling down my neck. What kind of message would it send if the new singer couldn't show up on time? But we made it with minutes to spare and stood like supplicants before a very polished receptionist behind a very large desk.

"Bella Morales for Ms. Lanier." I only hoped I didn't look as scared as I felt.

"Oh, yes, she's expecting you. Please have a seat."

We only waited about five minutes and I used the time to blot my face and compose myself. Then we were ushered into an impressive office, all mahogany and panoramic views.

Suzi was a tall, lean lady of indeterminate age, expertly coiffed and made up, dressed in jeans and stiletto heels. She jumped up and came around her desk to shake our hands, exuding down-home charm. On her desk, among teetering piles of paper, I saw a Mason jar of iced tea with a striped straw sticking out the top.

"Carol Lee," she called, "please bring my friends some iced tea, would you? Y'all like sweet tea, yes? Who doesn't, right? Now, Bella, sit down and tell me about your night at the Bluebird. I heard it was really something."

She was easy to talk to, fixing her gaze unwaveringly on my face, grimacing in sympathy when I described tripping on the steps to the stage, nodding to hear of Boyd's expert accompaniment, clapping her hands a couple of times when I spoke of the crowd's generous reaction.

"I know Boyd," she said. "He's a keeper. You can't do better than an honest Texas cowboy."

She stopped as she registered the look on Darren's face, and then finished smoothly, "Except for the boy from back home. But I can see you know that."

Darren relaxed visibly under her warm gaze.

"Mary was impressed," Suzi continued. "The Ladys just lost the opening act for their upcoming tour and she was at the Bluebird scouting for a replacement."

She mentioned the name of a famous but fading country star known to drown his talent in the whiskey river he sang about. "The only reason he agreed to open for a new band was that he was desperate for the money. But he couldn't stay sober even long enough to rehearse and now he's back in rehab for the umpteenth time. If you ask me, the Ladys should thank their lucky stars that it happened now instead of mid-tour. But it does leave them in a bind. Mary liked your old-time country style -- said it reminded her a little of Patsy Cline -- and she liked the contrast between the way you sing and the way you look. Not too many Latinas in country music, so you're a bit of a novelty. She asked me to see if you were interested in opening for them."

Suzi paused for breath and waited for my reaction, but I was so surprised I could only stare. An irrelevant thought crossed my mind: that's enough to make a fish stare. Mrs. Montez used to say that.

Suzi eyed me sternly. "Do I have to tell you

how rare it is for a performer without so much as a record to her name to get an offer to be an opening act, even as a last-minute replacement?"

"Oh my gosh, I'm just overwhelmed," I managed to get out. "I don't, I mean, I've never, are you sure they want *me*?"

"That's why you're here," Suzi said. "Now don't dither, honey. If you didn't have talent, you wouldn't have been asked. Are you interested or not?"

"Of course! Yes! I'm interested."

"Now, lookee here," Suzi continued in a getting-down-to-business voice, "the LadyBugs go on tour in one month, and they play in stadium venues all over the South, from Texas to Virginia. If you open for them, it will be like joining the Olympic swim team the day after you first swam across the pool. You've got four weeks to get ready, and I strongly advise that you spend the time working with a vocal coach, arranging your songs and taking guitar lessons. You'll have to figure out your own transportation because there ain't room on the girls' bus for you and your band. Scale is what you'll be paid. If any of the girls don't like you, or you don't live up to their expectations, you'll be out on your ear. You're getting a break the likes of which I've never seen in all my years as an agent. And speaking of that, I'd like to handle you."

I nodded eagerly. Of course, I wanted to be one of Suzi Lanier's clients; I'd never even dared to dream that big. But I winced inwardly at the word "band." *What band?*

"About here," Suzi said neutrally, "is when

new artists say they don't have money and ask if there's any way to get an advance on future earnings."

"That's one problem I don't have," I replied with a smile. As I recounted my lottery win, Suzi's eyes widened.

"Well, I swanee!" she said. "This is the first time I ever met anybody who actually won one of them things. I'd say it's a good omen. You're going to be lucky all through your life."

With that benediction ringing in our ears, Darren and I left Suzi's office carrying a contract that Suzi said was to be thoroughly vetted by my lawyer.

"You just bring it around whenever you sign it and leave it with Carol Lee. Unless you have questions or want to change anything. But it's a pretty standard contract."

Bouncing down the sidewalk like two kites, we returned to my hotel room and I immediately sat down with a yellow legal pad and a ballpoint pen and made a list:

Hire vocal coach
Find guitar teacher
Ask Boyd about band
Buy a tour bus
Rehearse

Darren was looking over my shoulder. "*Buy* a tour bus?" he said. "Just go out and buy a bus? Is that the way it's done?"

"It's the way I'm going to do it," I said. "I've got the money and I might as well jump in with both feet."

~*~

Boyd was a life-saver. He assembled a five-piece band, including himself, with a few phone calls. It seemed like it took him about half an hour.

"But that's because I know everybody in Nashville," he explained, "and I've worked with a lot of 'em. I know exactly who I want in a band."

He told me what the standard pay scale was and looked incredulous when I told him I meant to pay my musicians double the going rate.

"Why?" he asked. "We don't expect it."

"I want the best and I want loyalty. I can afford to pay for it."

I didn't go into the story of the lottery win; it seemed to be general knowledge anyhow.

"Who says you can't buy love?" he said, grabbing me in a bear hug. "You'll be the most popular new singer in history."

Boyd named the band Bowie County -- "because that's where I'm from" -- and we rehearsed every day. He arranged my original compositions and suggested some songs from other artists that I could cover. We'd be pretty much stuck with the same play list until our repertoire expanded but that was okay because we'd be in a new place every night.

Then we went shopping for a bus. That purchase was a real eye-opener. If you drive the highways around Nashville, you'll see the enormous buses that the top country stars call home during extended tours. With room for up to a dozen people to sleep, lounge, rehearse, shower and cook, many of them are larger than a double tractor-trailer. Darren and I went to a broker and I outlined my needs: six bunks, a bedroom, two bathrooms, and a kitchen.

As luck would have it, the broker had just taken possession of a bus I was told had belonged to a recently retired singer famous for her tours. She'd traveled in comfort: six spacious bunks for the band stacked tidily in tiers of three, a king-sized bed in a private bedroom with its own bathroom for Darren and me, another bathroom, a kitchen with refrigerator, microwave and ample storage space, white leather couches and captain's chairs, a built-in plasma television, and bins for instruments and road equipment in the back. The countertops were quartz, the floor was polished hardwood and the bathrooms were tiled in marble. It was a palace on wheels, with a palatial price: $385,000.

"Say I'm willing to pay that much for a bus," I said, "who's going to maneuver this monster on the road? Sure as heck not me!"

"Not me, either," Darren said. "Although, I *would* like to just try it and see what it feels like to drive it."

The broker assured us we could have our pick of professional drivers -- one more person on the payroll. I took a moment to wonder how far my $18 million would go.

"Let me think on it overnight," I said. I needed to talk to Boyd.

Boyd was familiar with that particular bus, he said, having toured briefly with the former owner. "It's a beauty," he said enthusiastically. "Runs like a dream, room for everybody, saves us a mint on hotel rooms. You couldn't do better. But hey, can you afford something that fancy?"

"Yup. I can always sell it. It's just like bricks and mortar, only on wheels, right? My concern is who will drive it."

"That's not a problem," Boyd said. "Joey is a tour bus driver as well as a guitar picker. That's how he makes ends meet. We've already hired him for Bowie County; pay him the going rate to drive the bus and you'll have a very happy camper."

"Isn't it a lot for one guy to handle, driving ten or twelve hours and then performing?" I asked.

"Ten hours is the limit the Department of Transportation allows one driver to be behind the wheel. The tour schedule has only one leg that would take a little bit longer than ten hours. I expect Joey would fudge a little bit there. You won't find a tougher bunch of guys than Nashville musicians. Getting too much sleep is actually bad for us. Let me talk to him."

Joey, predictably enough, was delighted to earn an extra $250 a day for driving, plus his already doubled salary for playing in Bowie County. He kissed his valid commercial driving license gleefully and went with us for a second look at the bus. He seemed so competent and at ease behind the wheel on our test drive that any misgivings I might have had were put to rest.

Darren went into business manager mode and entered into cut-throat negotiations over the price. The broker assured us that if the bus was brand-new ("and she looks it, don't she?") we'd have to add another hundred thousand to the price. Darren countered that paying cash should get us a healthy discount. I took a walk around the lot while they haggled. When he pronounced himself satisfied that a fair deal had been struck, I wrote out an enormous check and the bus was mine. I debated having my name painted on the side, but in the end I decided not to invite the wrath of the gods by such a display of confidence. I may have been able to buy a bus, but I was still very much on trial.

It was only later that it occurred to me to wonder if my bus was actually nicer than the one in which the LadyBugs traveled. Maybe I'd not made the most politically astute move, to out-bus my bosses. But it was too late for second thoughts; momentum was sweeping me along.

I worked hard during the weeks before the first concert. Darren was at my side for every step, going to rehearsals and lessons, stocking the bus, taking out insurance policies, setting up a basic payroll and bookkeeping system and handling the thousand and one details that -- who knew? -- undergirded a tour. What would I have done without him? The contrast between him and Miguel, who expected me to anticipate and grant his every whim, couldn't have been more pronounced.

The days were a hamster's wheel of activities and I didn't have time to think. But in that quiet space between sleeping and waking, when I could abandon my façade of false confidence, I acknowledged to myself that I was scared. I was getting what I always said I wanted but it was the difference between contemplating the high diving board from the ground, and bouncing up and down on it, ready to jump. *What if I fall flat? What if I don't like touring? What if the LadyBugs send me packing?*

What if I'm an imposter who doesn't deserve to succeed?

One what-if I never thought to add to the equation was Miguel.

Jim

Dr. Jim Miller remembered his first encounter with Marilyn Simmons and her dogs. He had entered the exam room on a busy day, clearing his mind for the next patients. Waiting for him was a woman who looked to be in her sixties, with a dog and a litter of puppies. True to his calling, Jim's first interest was in the animals. In a glance, he saw that the adult dog looked like a fairly typical mutt, about forty pounds and the yellowish buff color common to mixed breed dogs all over the world. The puppies were fat little balls of fur, obviously thriving.

"Hi, I'm Doctor Miller," he said, extending his hand to the woman

"Oh -- hi, I'm Marilyn Simmons -- no, *no,* Jack! Oh, I'm sorry, doctor, I'll clean it up."

"No need for that, if there's anything we're used to around here, it's pee. One of the techs will get it. Now, what have we got here? Let's start with mama."

He hoisted the adult dog up on the table and quickly assessed her needs: postpartum care, shots, worming, vitamins, a medicated shampoo and spaying so she wouldn't produce any more unplanned litters.

"She looks good -- a tad skinny from feeding all these little buggers," he said, "heart and lungs sound good, but it will be miraculous if she doesn't have heartworm. Cross your fingers."

With practiced fluidity, Jim wrapped a tourniquet around Sam's front leg, inserted a needle and drew blood into the syringe. Sam tried to pull back her leg but then submitted to the procedure resignedly. Jim handed off the vial of blood to a tech with a request to run a heartworm check and get right back with the results.

"She's a stray," Marilyn said. "I found her on the street just about to give birth so I took her home with me."

"Good for you," Jim said, smiling warmly at Marilyn. "I have a real soft spot in my heart for people who rescue dogs. Not enough of it going on in the world. Well done. Now, let's take a look at those puppies."

The rest of the visit was uneventful. Sam did not have heartworm and the puppies were thriving. Jim didn't think much more about his new patients until he began seeing Marilyn often as she brought in the pups for inoculations, spaying and neutering. He looked forward to spotting her name on the day's schedule. She seemed a pleasant person of modest means, and he worried a little bit about the charges she was incurring, although she always paid promptly and in cash.

After one particularly expensive visit in which all the puppies were micro chipped, he felt impelled to mention the cost.

"You don't have to pay for every visit at the time of service," he said. "I let my good patients run a tab, pay when it's convenient."

He was astounded when she told him she was a lottery winner. She certainly hadn't splashed out on clothes or jewelry or whatever people with big bucks buy, and he liked her even better for that. It certainly explained why she was so sanguine about the expense of adopting five dogs.

When she called in panic after the code enforcement officer's visit, the memory of her fortune popped into his head and he impulsively recommended she move to the country. Then he didn't see her for a couple of months and in the rush of day to day business, almost forgot about her. He felt a little zing of pleasure, hearing her voice again when she called to say she'd taken his advice, was in her new place in the country and had accumulated several stray dogs that needed veterinary attention.

"They need to be examined," she said, "but I don't know how I'll ever get them into the car. They act like they've never been in one but they must have had at least one car ride because someone dropped them off at the end of my driveway."

Jim thought she sounded flustered and, feeling sorry for her, offered to make a house call.

"We rescuers need to stick together," he said in response to her protests that it was asking too much of him to drive to the country.

So, on his next afternoon off he found himself driving slowly down a two-lane road, scanning mailboxes for names or house numbers. Finally, after making a U-turn and retracing his route, he saw a small black mailbox with an index card taped to the front: Simmons. He rolled up the gravel driveway until he came to a small, unprepossessing ranch house. Marilyn was sitting on the front porch, waiting for him.

"Well, hello," he said, getting out of the car and taking a few stiff steps to get the kinks out of his back and legs. "When you move to the country, you really move to the *country*!"

"Dr. Jim, it's so good of you to come all the way out here," Marilyn said, beaming as she walked to meet him.

A pack of dogs eddied around her legs. He recognized Sam and her half-grown pups, but the others were obviously the strays that Marilyn had called him about. He gave them a quick once-over and saw no glaring problems that demanded his immediate attention.

Instead, he turned in a slow circle to take in Marilyn's new home. In addition to the house, there was a detached garage that was clearly serving as a dog dorm. The green lawn gave way to a rolling meadow polka-dotted with yellow and white wildflowers. Beyond the meadow, a huge old tree flung its branches over a little creek that sparkled in the sun. The sound of water splashing over rocks made a counterpoint to the songs of a hundred birds. A faint smell of wood smoke hung in the air. What he didn't hear was traffic, car alarms, television commercials or ring-tones. What he didn't smell were exhaust fumes. What he didn't see were crowds of people rushing to and fro on concrete sidewalks.

He fell in love.

Jim had a dream, one he'd had for many years. He dreamed of living and working in the country, having a garden and growing some of his own food, caring for animals close to nature instead of city pavements. The little brook that tootled its way across Marilyn's acres, the canopy of old-growth trees, the wild flowers and the birdsong called to him, and they said, "Home."

Jim's house stopped feeling like a home when his wife of forty years died. He missed home and he missed Dotty. When she was around there was always music and laughter and the aroma of something good cooking. She was exhausting and sometimes irritating, he remembered that, too: talking non-stop, always with a hundred projects going at once, filling every room she entered with her presence. She delighted in teasing him, calling him Der Alte when she was feeling playful, which was most of the time. And then she was gone, pancreatic cancer moving fast to snuff out her life. That was two years ago.

He kept going, plodding along, one foot in front of the other, because he didn't know what else to do. It helped to be busy during the day with his practice, but his evenings were sunk in a lethargy that he refused to call depression because depression was weakness.

Just getting old, he told himself. *Not much excitement in the world for old folks.*

CHAPTER TWELVE

Marilyn

Living in the country several miles from the nearest store would mean I needed a better car. A pack of dogs who all loved to ride along meant I'd need a big, sturdy one. I bought the first van I saw with enough windows so that all five heads could hang out as five black noses worked blissfully in the breeze. I didn't care how much dog drool hit the windows or how much dog hair was upholstered to the seats. I wasn't going any place fancy.

The search for property was underway. I looked at several possibilities before I found one I loved. The house itself was pretty basic: a long, low, 1960s-era brick ranch that had not been updated, but I had no problem with linoleum floors and vinyl countertops, at least for a while. If the house was sound, cosmetic changes could always be made later. The land was the draw. I'd never seen a more beautiful setting and I wanted it with all my heart. But I forced myself to be practical. First order of business: get a home inspection.

I met the inspector at the property the following morning. He verified that the important things were in good shape: a fairly new roof, recently added heat pump for both heating and air conditioning, PVC pipes and an up-to-code circuit box. I was looking around as he spoke. In fact, I was turning in a full circle. The land was so beautiful.

It lay at the base of a small mountain, a ten acre plot that contained a busy little stream, enormous old shade trees and open meadows lush with wild flowers. At the bottom of the long gravel driveway was a paved two-lane road lined with goldenrod and Queen Anne's Lace. There were no near neighbors, so only the birds, my dogs and the occasional raccoon or deer would keep me company. I gazed and gazed, but like a star-struck lover, I couldn't think of one thing to do to make it better. It was perfect.

I made a cash offer for the full asking price that day. The elderly seller needed money to move into a retirement home and I needed -- *needed* -- to live in that peaceful space. We quickly struck a deal and each of us felt we'd gotten the best of it.

I'd carefully checked the county zoning rules and found a lot of regulations about vicious animals but not a word about the allowable numbers of dogs per residence. I took that to mean there were no restrictions. Even though I was pretty sure I wasn't breaking any rules this time, the first thing I did was to have the entire property surrounded by a sturdy fence so the dogs could run free without straying from my property. No sense annoying my new neighbors.

Cash greases wheels, so in a dizzyingly short time, I was established in my new place. Eventually, the kitchen and bathrooms would be gutted and replaced, the old hardwood floors refinished and I'd have someone see about the land over the septic tank that got swampy when it rained hard. All in good time. The important thing was just being here.

The dogs were ecstatic with freedom. They chased rabbits, splashed in the stream and took long, snoring naps in the sunshine. They also created a lot of work for me. I did morning duty with a pooper-scooper, scrubbed their food bowls, hauled their big bags of kibble and swept up enough hair to stuff a mattress every day. All that I could handle easily enough, but I still needed somebody to mow the grass and the meadows.

I stopped regularly at a farm stand down the road, manned during the summer by a teenage boy selling what he told me were his grandpa's vegetables and his grandma's homemade pickles. We fell into conversation one day when I went to buy the first of the sweet corn.

"It's my summer job," he said. "I'd rather a 'been a life-guard at the pool, but those jobs got grabbed up fast. I'm saving for a car."

"Do you want a little extra work?" I asked.

"Hmmm. Depends."

" I need somebody to cut grass."

"What kind of lawnmower do you have?" he asked cagily. Clearly he wasn't going to allow himself to be overworked.

"I don't have one yet. Maybe you could tell me the best kind to get."

He looked interested for the first time. Boys and machines.

"You'd probably want a riding mower," he said. "Toro makes good ones, or John Deere if you want a great big 'un. Where did you say you live? Did you buy the old Brewster place?"

"Yes. Right down the road. You wouldn't have far to go and I'd just need you to cut the grass once a week."

"How much would you pay?"

"Well, I have a pretty big lawn, and then there are several acres of meadow. How much do you think would be fair?"

A happy, acquisitive light shone in his eyes.

"Uh, les' see. You must have about ten-twelve acres, not all of it in grass, a' course. It would probably take me three or four hours. Let's say twenty-five dollars an hour," he peeked at me to gauge my reaction. "What about a hundred dollars total?"

"Okay."

"Okay? Do you mean it? You don't think that's too much?"

"It sounds fair. If you do a good job, you'll be worth every penny. If you don't, I'll find somebody else."

"I'll do a good job, I promise, Mrs., Miss--"

"Marilyn Simmons. Please call me Marilyn. And you are?"

"Michael, ma'am, but folks call me Little Mike because my dad is Big Mike. When do you want me to start?"

"The grass is growing as we speak, Little Mike. I'll go on to the Ace Hardware and pick out a mower. If they can deliver it today, you can mow tomorrow. Does that suit you?"

"Yes, ma'am, Miz Simons, I mean, Marilyn. I'll come to your house after I close the stand. Grandpa likes me to stay open until the evening commuters come through, so it will be about seven, but there's still lots of daylight left then. Okay?"

"Okay."

We shook on it. I could tell Little Mike thought he'd struck it rich; he couldn't know how little that hundred dollars a week meant to me, and how happy I was to have some help.

He showed up on time the next evening, spent a few minutes admiring the new bright red lawnmower, then cranked it up and hopped aboard. Soon I was inhaling the perfume of freshly-cut grass. He couldn't get it all done before the light was gone, so he promised to finish the next day. I gave him a glass of lemonade and he sat with me on the porch for a few minutes to watch the sun set.

"Let me pay you today," I said.

"No, no," he said, waving my money away, "wait until I'm all done and then see if you're satisfied with the job."

He was proving to be a nice boy, Little Mike was, and a good worker. And just maybe, my first new friend.

~*~

We may have been living in doggy paradise, but I was lonely. I'd come to count on my urban strolls with the dogs for the human contact they provided. Now I had no near neighbors and no park full of friendly faces. My interactions were limited to the clerks in the grocery and pet stores, Little Mike on the lawnmower, and, of course, my frequent visits to Dr. Jim's office. I'll confess: those visits were more frequent than might have been strictly medically necessary, but he was always welcoming and patient with me and my rowdy pack.

I got to know the staff in the veterinary office. Marlene was the "up-front girl," as she called herself, and we always chatted while I waited my turn.

"You know, Dr. Jim really likes you," she said, with a meaningful look. "He's a widower. His wife, Dotty, died a couple years back. Dr. Jim's kinda been in a funk since then. But he perks right up when he knows you're coming in."

"He's a very nice man," I said primly. "I'm sure he must have a lot of friends."

I wasn't about to get caught up in an embarrassing match-making effort, not after my speed-dating debacle. Besides, I liked Jim, too, more than I wanted him or anyone else to know. I was old-fashioned, not to mention woefully out of practice at the man/woman thing, and as far as I was concerned, it was up to the man to make the first move.

~*~

One afternoon I was roused from a guilty half-nap by a cacophony of barking dogs, followed by a knock on the door. On my step just outside the screen door stood a stranger. The first things I noticed were the tattoos that emerged from his ragged T-shirt, circled his neck and covered his shaved scalp. His arms, too, wore sleeves of colorful ink. I shivered to see the piercings in his nose, lip and eyebrow. An old car was parked out by the road; he'd walked up to the door instead of using the driveway. No wonder I hadn't heard him. The back of my neck prickled as I remembered how isolated I was.

The dogs reluctantly stopped barking at my repeated commands, but they made a silent circle around him, keeping a wary distance. Sam's hackles were raised, her ears and tail straight up. Her endearing smile was absent. The pups copied her stance and demeanor, looking edgy and scared. The man kept glancing uneasily over his shoulder at them.

"Yes? Can I help you?"

"Nice place you got here. Live here by yourself?"

"Uh, no, my... husband is here. And, and my son. My grown son."

"Oh, yeah?" Don't see 'em. Just the one car. Quiet guys, I guess. I ran out of gas. Got any?"

"No, I'm afraid not. There's a gas station about a mile down the road, though."

"How about giving me a ride?" He glanced at my van in the driveway.

"No. I'm -- busy."

Belatedly I tried to hook the screen door, just as he reached for the handle. With a jerk, the door was pulled from my grasp.

"Well, then I guess I'll just come in and wait until you're not busy."

I screamed, a good loud movie-type scream. I always wondered if I would be able to make a sound if I ever found myself in danger: yes, I could.

The scream galvanized Sam, who charged and sank her strong teeth into the stranger's leg. She shook her head, driving her long eyeteeth in deeper, pulling him backward while he swore and swatted at her. I wasn't about to let my dog fight alone. I grabbed the porch broom and began beating the man anywhere I could land a blow. He lost his balance and sprawled in the dirt, which the half-grown pups took as their invitation to join in the fray. A big stray who had shown up only yesterday and looked like she had some pit bull in her, took the entire top of his head in her large mouth. I managed a good whack at his crotch with the broom handle, and when he curled up in pain, dogs piled on his back, snapping at his face and neck. Sam never let go of his leg. Finally, through all the tumult, I realized that he was begging.

"Call 'em off, lady, call 'em off! Just let me get outta here."

I did, with some difficulty because the dogs were in a frenzy. He scrambled to his feet, blood trickling down his temple, and made a shambling, running retreat to his car, pursued all the way by barking canines. He threw himself into the driver's seat, gunned the engine and shot forward, tires screeching.

I allowed my shaky legs to lower me to the porch floor and the dogs crowded around. The youngsters were full of excitement and self-congratulation, but Sam leaned heavily against me, trembling. There was blood on her mouth and I gently wiped at it with my shirttail. It was not in her nature to be vicious and it had cost her something.

I reached for my phone, ready to dial 911 to report an intruder. But then the thought of Sam's bloody mouth stopped my hand. What if the police deemed her a vicious dog? There was plenty in the County Code about that! What if Animal Control came and hauled Sam off to quarantine, to languish until they decided she didn't have rabies? I remembered a news report about a police officer shooting a homeowner's pet because he felt threatened. A dog with a bloody mouth could certainly be construed as threatening. No, better not involve the authorities. Just let it go and hope that my intruder didn't become someone else's intruder. I didn't feel like a very good citizen that day.

After that, our patch of paradise didn't seem so much like Eden anymore. I locked the doors when I was in the house, and maintained a constant vigil when I was outside, feeling the lack of near neighbors even more. There were no reassuring houses just a shout away, no lights shining across the dark fields. The nights seemed endless, made of smothering ebony velvet relieved only by the moon and the stars. I had trouble sleeping. I wondered, during those long, dark hours, if I had made a terrible mistake.

CHAPTER THIRTEEN

Star

Here's what I had to do: resign from my job, hire a moving crew, engage an interior decorator to get the new house ready for us, and find a cleaning crew to get the old house ready for Jane. Dazed by the presence of so much help, I stood by to make the decisions that only Rowan or I could make and let the crews do their work. It was hard to get used to; Rowan and I had always done everything ourselves.

We took the things that were priceless to us -- antiques and family heirlooms that I knew had no real value for anyone else. Everything else we left for Jane and the kids. The decorator did all the shopping for the new house, and presented us with choices between three or four items, rather than hundreds. In a remarkably short time, both houses were ready for their new occupants. We moved out one day and Jane and her family moved in the next. By the weekend, we were all getting settled in our new homes.

I kept my promise and contacted my friend in the local hospital's Human Resources department. Jane was invited to submit her application and was promptly hired as a phlebotomist.

"It's about as entry-level as you can get," she said, when she called to tell me about it, "but I don't care, it's a start. And the hospital has a wonderful day care center right on campus for the little ones, subsidized so it costs less than anywhere else I could place them. I've got Julia and the twins in school and they seem to be making a good adjustment. They don't have to be ashamed of living in a shelter anymore. Julia wants to have a slumber party so her new friends can see her room. Star, we will never be able to repay you for what you've done for us."

"No repayment needed. Rowan and I are delighted things are working out so well for you. Most of it is due to your own hard work."

But Jane was full of gratitude that we knew she needed to express. So we accepted every invitation to birthday parties, family dinners and school programs. Rowan, especially, was in love with the children. Joy came running at the sound of his voice, enveloping his knees in her pudgy little arms until he lifted her to his shoulders. The boys, Jonas and Jacob, enlisted his aid with fort-building and story problems. Julia baked him cookies. Jennifer "read" to him from books she'd memorized. I could see that they filled a void in Rowan's life; a void I had almost forgotten was there.

On weekends we'd often invite the children to our house if Jane had to work, or if she had the days off, to give her a chance to get some housework done without all the interruptions. We had a little guest cottage by the pool, and the girls quickly commandeered it as a play house. While the boys dived and splashed like otters, the girls dressed up in my old clothes and held tea parties. Rowan was an honored and enthusiastic guest at both events, and I watched the love grow between him and the children. It worried me. They were not ours.

Rowan was cut out for fatherhood, but he'd been headed for a different kind of it. He was going to be a priest. That he was to be the first African-American priest ordained from his parish was a huge deal. He told me how he struggled, how he tried to reconcile his desire for a family with his vow of celibacy, how he hated to disappoint all those who had supported him. But he couldn't do it and when I first met him, he was a priestly drop-out. I liked his old-fashioned manners, his kind eyes, and his sincerity. There was absolutely no flash to Rowan. He said he liked my soft heart and wide tolerance. Eventually, he said that meeting me made leaving seminary worthwhile. I took that as a great compliment, because I knew how hard it had been for him.

"In the end, I just couldn't let go of the idea of having a family," he said. "I don't want to miss out on all that. My folks were great parents; I want to be one, too. The deeper I got into my vocation, the more I realized I'm not cut out for the celibate life. Oh, it's not sex so much -- although that's very nice -- it's the whole family thing, the interconnectedness that only comes in a family. I want that, Star."

Of course, I wanted it, too, and with Rowan. And so we married. We expected to have children. We wanted them, tried for them, and I know Rowan prayed for them. It didn't happen. After a year, we made the rounds of fertility specialists, did all the humiliating things that were supposed to provide answers.

"I can't see any reason why you have not conceived," the last specialist said. "Sometimes conception just doesn't occur and we can't say why. I'd advise you to make peace with your lives as they are. Sometimes when people just relax, it happens. I'm sorry; I don't have any other answer."

But it didn't happen and it was heartbreaking, especially for Rowan. But we told ourselves to accept reality and make the best life we could. As the years passed, having children of our own receded into the background in my mind. What we had was enough for me. Until Jane and her children entered our lives, I thought it had become enough for Rowan, too.

~*~

We were curled up on the sofa together, watching the eleven o'clock news, drowsy and ready for sleep, when a familiar face flashed on the screen.

"That's Jane!" we said together. We sat up.

"Following up on a report of shots fired, police today found two bodies in a unit at the Store-It-All facility on National Highway. They have been identified as Jane Kaufman and James Kaufman. Preliminary evidence indicates a murder/suicide. A police spokesperson declined further comment about an ongoing investigation."

Rowan's eyes met mine, and I knew that I looked as horrified as he did.

"The kids," he said, already untangling himself from me and the afghan over us. "We've got to get the kids."

"But where would they be?" I asked. "They wouldn't be home alone, would they?"

"The police probably turned them over to the Department of Family and Children's Services," Rowan said. "We have to go to the police station; we have to go now."

As he spoke, he was stuffing his feet into his shoes and grabbing his car keys. I hurried after him, snagging my purse as we ran from the house, barely making it into the car before he threw it in reverse and backed down the driveway. The ride into town took twenty minutes, or twenty days, or twenty years. We skidded to a stop in the parking lot of the main police station, and again I had to run to keep up with Rowan.

"The Kaufman children," he said to the desk sergeant. "We just heard about their mother's death. Where are the kids?"

He gave us that cool, assessing look that cadets learn first thing in the police academy.

"Are you relatives?" he asked.

"We're friends; landlords," Rowan said. "Friends, really. We want to see the children. Please."

Of course, that didn't happen, not right then. The children were indeed in protective custody or foster care or whatever the official jargon was. We had to wait until the next day and then meet with a social worker and convince her that we were who we said we were.

"These kids have had their mother taken and their world turned upside down," Rowan said, "They need to see people they know and trust."

"Do you know if there are any other relatives?" the social worker asked. "They can't give us any information about an extended family, not even the oldest girl."

"I never heard Jane speak of relatives," I said, realizing for the first time that this was true. "She said her husband left her. That's all I knew about her life before we got to know her."

"And what exactly was your relationship with Mrs. Kaufman and her family?"

"I met her when she applied for Section Eight housing, where I used to work. There was nothing available for her family and I put them up in a motel out of my own pocket. That's something I shouldn't have done, as a city employee, but they were homeless and I couldn't stand it. Later, I came into a lot of money and made a house available to Jane. She just started working at the hospital. The three older kids are in school and the two little ones go to daycare."

After we produced papers and signed papers and read papers, we were allowed, finally, to see them. Julia's face was the color of a bleached bone as she herded her brothers and sisters into the little interview room. Jonas and Jacob looked too scared even for tears, but the little girls immediately burst into wails when they saw us. Joy ran to Rowan and he picked her up with one arm, while extending the other arm for Jenny. I gathered Julia and the boys to me. We all cried.

Eventually we settled down and Joy fell asleep on Rowan's shoulder, her thumb in her mouth. Jonas and Jacob were easily distracted by the IPod in my shoulder bag and immediately embarked on a game of Angry Birds. Jenny sat on my lap, grasping my blouse as if to hold me down.

"Julia, do you know what has happened?" I asked.

"They told me Mom's dead," she said. No ten-year-old should have to say those words as bleakly as she said them. "Dad came to the house yesterday afternoon. We were surprised because Mom said she didn't know where he was, that maybe he'd gone far away. When we all lived together, he used to get real mad at Mom and hit her. The worst time, Mom took us to a batter… battery women's shelter. When we went back to our house, he wasn't there, and all our stuff was gone. Our furniture and clothes and toys. Mom called the landlord, but he said we couldn't go back in our house because the rent wasn't paid. So then we had to sleep in shelters.

But Dad talked nice to Mom when he found us. He said he'd saved our stuff and put it in a storage unit, but he couldn't pay the rent and the landlord was going to open it and throw everything out. Dad said, 'This is all you'll ever have. If you don't get this stuff today, it'll be gone.'

At first she said no, she wouldn't go with him. She said he should tell her where it was and she'd go by herself. But then he said the bus didn't go there and he'd give her a ride."

"I would have taken her," Rowan said softly.

"I know, I said that. She didn't want to bother

you all the time."

Julia stared into space for long moments.

"She said, 'Julia, watch the little ones, I'll be back in an hour.' But she didn't come and we got hungry. I fixed Cheerios for everyone. Then we watched TV until the policemen knocked. I was afraid to open the door, because I'm never s'posed to when Mom's not home, but they said, 'Open up, police" so I did. Then some ladies came and made us go with them." She gave a huge gulp and fell silent.

Into the silence, Rowan spoke. "It's going to be all right. We're trying our best to get you out of foster care but it may take a while so you'll need to be very brave. Your mom would want you to be brave and to be good."

"What will happen to us?" Julia asked.

"We hope you'll come live with us," Rowan said.

Darren

It was a lot of work, getting Bella's show on the road. I was busy all day with the details she didn't have time for. She rehearsed with the band and had her voice and guitar lessons while I handled the business end of things. It was assumed that I was Bella's manager, although we had no formal agreement.

Most nights, we'd crawl back to our hotel suite, order room service and fall into an exhausted sleep. Bella was invited to return to the Bluebird Café and she honed her act there, performing a couple of times a week. Each time she got technically better, but I thought she never equaled the electric excitement of her first appearance.

Something was bothering me but I didn't want to tell her about it. A couple of times I thought I saw Miguel. Once in the hotel lobby, another time on the street, but the glimpses I had were so fleeting that I wasn't completely sure it was him. Finally I came upon him propping up the bar at the Bluebird and confronted him. He looked rough; dark circles under his bloodshot eyes, hair that needed a barber and a pervasive aroma of tequila, cigarettes and clothes that needed a trip to the washer.

"Miguel. What are you doing in Nashville?"

"It's a free country, man; I can be anywhere I want to be."

"Are you by any chance thinking you can get to Bella? Because I'm here to tell you that you can't."

"Is that right, Mr. Big Shot? You think because you're sleeping with her now, that makes you special and you can keep her away from me? Bella is into me, man. We just had a little misunderstanding. If I get ten minutes with her, she takes me back. It's just that simple."

"Listen, Miguel, don't make a mistake here. Bella's moved on. She's finished with you. Her life is going in a different direction now and she has no room for you in it."

"Yeah, well, fuck you."

With a scripted Miguel sneer and swagger, he dodged around me and disappeared into the crowd. I searched for him for a few minutes, but then Bella's act was announced and I went in to watch her. I didn't forget him, though, or his implied threat. After a lot of thought, I decided not to tell Bella. She was already stressed to the max getting ready for the tour. She didn't need one more thing.

Bella

"Querida."

Only one person ever called me that. I spun around and there he was, in the lobby of my hotel. For once, Darren was nowhere in sight.

"Miguel. I'm surprised to see you here," I said, summoning all the nonchalance at my command.

He looked as though he'd been sleeping in his car and eating a lot of fast food. The sleekness and finicky grooming he'd had when he lived with me were gone. He looked smaller and seedier. Somehow that made him seem less threatening.

"I've been seeing you, querida. I've been watching you sing at the Bluebird. You're looking good. Muy bonita."

He gave me one of his patented smoldering looks. How had I ever thought he was sexy? He seemed more like Snidely Whiplash than Antonio Banderas now.

"So, shall we get a drink, querida? Catch up on old times?"

"After what you did to my apartment? You have more guts than a twelve-string," I said, making for the elevator.

He slipped in beside me as the doors closed. Uh oh, big mistake, stupid me. We were alone in a little box. Instantly he was on me, pinning my arms, pushing me against the wall.

"Miguel! Stop right now," I said, struggling in his grasp.

"You know you want it, querida," he said, pushing his knee between my legs.

"Get off me, I mean it! I'll scream!"

The tone signaling that the elevator door was opening peeled Miguel away. A middle-aged couple entered the cab, looking curiously at us – me breathless and red-faced, Miguel looking innocently at the ceiling.

"Everything all right here?" the man asked.

"My... friend... here was just saying goodbye. We won't see each other again after today," I said.

Miguel glared at me, not bothering to smolder this time. The hatred in his face was blatant and the woman moved closer to me. When she and her husband reached their floor, she took my arm without a word and walked me off with them. What I hoped was my last glimpse of Miguel was his angry face disappearing behind the closing doors.

"I don't want to criticize a friend of yours, dear," my rescuer said, "but if you were my daughter, I'd tell you to be careful of that one. He looked dangerous to me. Are you going to be okay now?"

"Yes, ma'am, thank you. My room is just one floor up and my boyfriend is waiting for me there. I can take the stairs."

"We're going to wait right here at the bottom," the man said. "If anything scares you, give a good, loud scream."

I thanked them again and ran up the steps two at a time, escaping to the safety of our room and

Darren. I decided I wouldn't tell him about Miguel, not right now.

Darren

I knew something was wrong, but I let her take her own time to tell me. When she finally did, I understood for the first time the expression "seeing red." I believe I could and would have killed Miguel if he'd been in front of me.

"Darren, don't look like that!" Bella begged. "It's over; there was no real harm done. He just scared me. I haven't seen him since and I'm only telling you now so you can help me be on the lookout for him when we're touring."

"So you think he'll be back?"

"I don't know. I never could predict what Miguel would do. At the time, that was part of the attraction, but I've lost my taste for bad boys."

She gave me that smile that makes me melt.

" I know you've got my back. I just want to concentrate on my performances and not blow this opportunity because of a jerk like Miguel."

Okay, I took that as my marching order and made sure she was never alone. I worried about smothering her, but she was totally preoccupied with rehearsals, and sometimes I wasn't sure she even noticed me except as background. Being in her background was more than I could have ever dreamed of, but now I wanted more. I wanted Bella to love me.

CHAPTER FOURTEEN

Star

And just like that, the little sealed unit that was Rowan and Star became a family with five children. I wasn't so sure about it. When Rowan and I talked it over later, I said so.

"We've got a great life now," I said. "At least, *I* think so. Who knows what needs and problems these poor kids are going to have. Can we cope with it? We don't know anything about raising kids, let alone troubled ones."

"I know," Rowan said. "It scares me, too. But I already feel like they are ours. This sounds flaky and woo-woo, I know, but I wonder if Jane came into our lives so we'd be here for this moment. We can afford to take on five children, which is more than most people could do." Rowan stopped and looked pained. "Here I am, spending your money, after all my big talk about it being *your* money."

"Rowan, how many times do I have to say it? The money is ours, just like everything else in our lives. We're a team and we share the good and the bad. Please knock it off; you're getting to be a real pain about it."

Rowan nodded ruefully. "Okay, okay. If I had won the lottery, I would never have thought for one minute it was all mine, and I know you are a far more generous person than I am. I don't know why I keep casting you in the role of Ebenezer Scrooge. From now on, I promise: it's *our* money."

"And you want to spend some of it raising Jane's children," I prompted, to get him back to the subject at hand.

"Taking care of them wouldn't be all on you," he said. "You've been telling me that I should quit working; well, now I will. I want to be here with them. Maybe this *is* our family, our chance at last to be parents."

"I didn't know you still missed being a parent so much," I said, with a lump in my throat. I felt hurt, although a rational part of my mind told me that was absurd. "I thought we were happy, just the two of us."

"Of course we were -- are. Look, if you don't want this, we'll forget it. We can still help the kids even if we don't raise them."

"I need to take a breath," I said. "Could you give me twenty-four hours to talk to my Mom and get my head together?"

"Of course."

~*~

I was at Mom's door early the next morning. She was alone in the house, Dad having gone fishing. In a corner of my mind, I registered with satisfaction that my Dad had time to go fishing now that he didn't have to work anymore, and my Mom could linger over coffee in her bathrobe instead of scrambling out to a job.

"Star, what brings you over so early?" Mom asked.

"It's Jane's kids," I said, without preamble. "Rowan wants to adopt them."

"Yes, that's what I expected. What's the problem?"

"Well -- five children, Mom! I don't know anything about raising kids and then to just jump into it with *five*. And white children, at that, so we'd have the interracial thing going on. How would I cope? And it would change everything. Our lives would be different from now on, and maybe not in a good way."

"You and Rowan wanted children once, didn't you?"

"Yes, but our own baby would have been different. Starting from scratch, I would have learned as I went along. Someone else's half-grown kids -- I don't know if I could do it."

Mom smiled. She patted my hand exactly the way she used to do when I came home from school full of tales of fifth-grade slights and schoolyard spats.

"Oh, I know you could do it, Star. You're made for it, and so is Rowan. You love those kids, right? Does it matter to *you* that they aren't African-American?"

"No, of course not. And I do love them -- who wouldn't? They're wonderful children. I'm just scared."

"Exactly. You're just scared. And what did I always tell you to do when you were little and got scared?"

"Hold my head up and look whatever scared me right in the face," I recited with a smile.

"I'm not telling you what to do, now," Mom said. "All I'm saying is take a good look at what's scaring you. One thing I know for sure is that you can handle whatever comes your way. And anyway, you already know what you're going to do; you just haven't said it to yourself yet."

As usual, Mom was right. I went home to Rowan. He was in the back yard, weeding furiously along the fence line. Yard work had always been his stress-reliever and those weeds didn't stand a chance while he waited for me and my decision.

"Rowan," I said, when he looked up. "I talked to Mom. I've got an answer for you now."

Rowan pulled me against his chest. I could hear his heart thumping away reliably -- his big, loving heart that had room in it for five children that were not his own, were not even of his race. How could I say no? With trepidation, with excitement, with love -- I said yes.

~*~

First there was a funeral to plan. The little ones would probably not remember it, but we thought it important that the older children had a memory of saying a formal goodbye to their mother.

Jane's body was cremated, and the funeral home made their smallest chapel available to us. We hired an organist and a florist to fill the little space with music and flowers. The sun shone that day, for which I was thankful. Funerals seem so much worse when the sky weeps. The brief ceremony was attended only by us, Jane's children and their social worker. Each of the children spoke of their mother, sharing a memory, a special time, what they loved about her.

"She taught me to cook and sew," Julia said through tears. "She French-braided my hair. I could tell her everything."

"She always gave us stuff to eat, even when we didn't have a house," Jacob said.

Jonas added, "And she played Go Fish with us."

"I love Mama," Jennifer said, with the simplicity of a four-year-old.

"Mama?" echoed Joy, looking around for her.

Jane's ashes were interred in a memorial rose garden on the grounds of the hospital where she had been so proudly, albeit briefly, employed. The children would be able to visit her grave and remember that.

Then there was the matter of their father. I favored letting the state put him in a pauper's grave. Rowan reminded me that, no matter what horrible crime he had committed, he would always be a part of his children.

"What we do with him now will color the way they think about him for the rest of their lives," he said. "I won't make one single excuse for him, but I will see to it that he is treated with decency."

Only the older children attended the second

service. They didn't speak this time, just listened as an unfamiliar minister read some scripture and spoke a few words meant to be comforting. The ashes were buried in a cemetery far from Jane's garden. Finally, with both parents laid to rest, the orphaned children could begin to heal.

Bella

Elation filled the inside of the bus like helium. We were off to our first stop, Atlanta, where the LadyBugs were scheduled to play the legendary Fox Theater. Taking a look at the Moorish masterpiece on Peachtree Street made my knees knock together. Darren kept busy reassuring me.

"You know you can do this. You blew the doors off the Bluebird Café. The Fox is just another venue, only now you've gotten even better with all the lessons and rehearsals. It will be a triumph and everybody will be so proud and delighted for you."

Darren was indispensable. I found myself turning to him first for just about everything. I knew he loved me. I loved him, too, but maybe not as much. I wasn't sure how I felt about him, or how fair it was, not knowing, to let him carry so much of the load. But there's no time for soul-searching when you're on tour. The band and I rehearsed as the bus lumbered along the interstate for the four-hour drive between Nashville and downtown Atlanta, and in our state of giddy nerves, we thought we sounded pretty darn good.

Arriving at the Fox, parking in the designated parking lot and getting ourselves and our instruments backstage, I was thankful that the members of Bowie County were far more experienced than I. They'd all played backup on tours before and went about their business with assurance and good humor.

We assembled on time and on cue for our first run-through. The lights, the marks on the stage that I had to hit, the sound-checks were all new to me and I felt mentally exhausted by the time our rehearsal was over. Darren escorted me back to the bus, brewed me a cup of hot tea laced with honey and a drop of Jack Daniels, and tucked me into bed for a nap. I surprised myself by actually dozing off for a few minutes.

And then it was show time. Dressed in my trademark jeans, tee-shirt and cowboy boots, stage makeup applied, hair artfully tossed over one shoulder, I peeked through the curtain as the house filled. My stomach contained a forest full of butterflies and my head felt thick and hot, like I'd been out in the sun too long. If Darren hadn't kept his arm around me, I might have run right out the backstage door.

Then, with a gentle push between my shoulders, he propelled me out into the blinding lights as Bowie County hit the first licks of my opening number. I plucked the mike from the stand, planted my feet and sang. We were on.

It's impossible to judge a performance when you're in the thick of it, but after my initial nervousness settled, I thought we were doing okay. The audience was there to hear the LadyBugs and they didn't know me from Adam, but they were generous with their applause. After a couple of numbers, I realized I was having fun. I relaxed, smiled, moved around a little bit. Once again, applause hit my bloodstream like a drug and once again, I couldn't get enough of it. When our set was over, I left the stage in a state of euphoria.

"I want to do it again!" I said to Darren as he enveloped me in his arms.

Marilyn

Sam brought him to me. She scratched on the screen door and when I came out, she showed me, sheltering in her wake, a large yellow dog with one milky blue eye. He looked exhausted and beat-up, but his ragged tail wagged a timid hello. Sam turned and licked his face, then smiled at me. Clearly, she was introducing her new friend to her old friend. The puppies, now almost fully grown, circled excitedly, darting in for a courageous sniff at the stranger.

"Where did you come from?" I asked.

Predictably, he didn't answer. I got out the bag of dog food and poured a bowlful, which I placed on the step with a pan of water. The pups thought it was for them, despite having full stomachs from their breakfast an hour ago, but Sam warned them off with a growl. The stranger lowered his head to the bowl, nibbled a bite and then gobbled, pausing to look around for interlopers every minute or two. He drank long and deeply, then turned around three times and plumped to the ground with a groan. Instantly, he was asleep. Sam lay down next to him, fixing the pups with a warning eye until they gave up and went about their business, leaving the grown-ups alone.

I named him Stranger and of course, I let him stay. There must have been some kind of underground telegraph that spread the news that my place was a good spot for dumping dogs. It was true, since I couldn't turn them away.

I seethed with anger at the callous owners who could discard family pets when they became inconvenient. The dogs' puzzled, forlorn faces, not to mention the signs of fear and hunger and abuse which some of them had clearly endured, made me weep. Sam was the house mother, gentling the fearful ones, taming the fierce ones, disciplining the unruly ones. My pack grew.

I called Dr. Jim. "What can I do with so many dogs?" I wailed. "I can't even bring them in for checkups, there are too many for me to handle."

"I'll come to you," he said.

And he did, bringing his vet bag and his own dog, a beautiful mahogany Irish setter named Siobhan. All one long afternoon -- his only day off -- he took temperatures, peered into ears, clipped toenails, gave injections and inspected teeth. At the end of the day, he could hardly straighten up after spending so many hours working on the ground.

"You really need an examining table out here," he said. "And a big sink with spray attachments for baths, and a few crates for the ones that need to be kept quiet."

"In other words, I need a vet's office," I said.

"Yeah, I guess you do. And, Marilyn, I hate to

tell you this, but you probably also need some kind of license or something if you're going to care for this many dogs. You're going to get into the same trouble with the county zoning ordinances that you had in the city. Are you going to continue to take in strays?"

"I don't mean to, but what else can I do when people put them out of cars at the end of my drive? Sam goes and gets them, and I can't turn them away."

"That's what I figured you'd say." He was silent for a few minutes, then spoke hesitantly. "I don't know if I should say this, but I've been thinking about it. You could form your own non-profit rescue organization. Incorporate as a 501(c)(3) and take out liability insurance. Get the proper permit and put up a small building to house and care for the dogs. Advertise for volunteers to help out. Have a fund-raiser, get the community involved, take dogs to adoption events, form a board of directors...."

Jim's face was alight with enthusiasm, but his voice trailed off as he took in my horrified expression.

"I wouldn't know where to begin," I said. "It's a great idea -- for someone -- but it's overwhelming."

"It must sound like climbing Mount Everest," Jim said. "I've been thinking about something like this for years, so I've already hiked through the foothills. Look, let me help you. I could be your medical director and I know a couple of my vet techs would jump at the chance to do rescue work. I'll bet, when the word spreads, you'll have plenty of helpers.

Facilities will have to be built, and you'll need a good lawyer and an accountant to keep meticulous books. Even if you only spend your own money, your records need to be absolutely transparent if other people are involved in any way, even as volunteers."

He ran out of breath and took a deep one. I did, too, to steady my nerves at such a daunting prospect.

"But, Marilyn," Jim continued, "do *you* want to do this? I realize I'm talking about *my* dream, one I've never had the money to make come true. Now that I'm nearing retirement age, I'm trying to think how I want to spend my time after I no longer go to an office. I see a wonderful opportunity to work on a cause close to my heart -- rescuing dogs -- but is it something *you* want to do? I can pretty well guarantee it will consume you and take your life in new directions. Your days will be full of needy dogs and urgent work. Maybe you want a quieter life in retirement. You need to think about it."

I thought of how lonely and yes, afraid, I felt in my remote and quiet place; then I imagined it swarming with enthusiastic volunteers, maybe youngsters like Little Mike. I would need to get up early in the morning and get busy because people and animals were depending on me. I pictured the dogs that washed up at my house on a sea of neglect and how wonderful it would be to place them in new forever homes. I thought about all my lottery money doing some good in the world, one dog at a time.

"I don't need to think about it," I said. "It sounds like heaven."

Jim

Jim's dream, blurted out impulsively, took a giant step toward reality. He looked at Marilyn with new eyes, seeing that her move to the country had changed her. She seemed taller, slimmer and more confident. He couldn't remember -- was her hair always that russet color?

He took to timing his visits close to dinner when he discovered that Marilyn liked to cook. Soon he came to count on a delicious meal in her kitchen almost every evening. Marilyn even liked Siobhan, muddy paws and all. Slow down, Jim cautioned himself, this is all moving too fast.

But he couldn't stay away. He headed for Marilyn's house after work almost every day and on weekends. It made for long hours and sometimes Jim pushed himself through a thick fog of fatigue. Caught up in his dream, he willed his body to keep going, deaf and blind to all but the exciting possibilities he saw unfolding before him.

He was nailing chicken wire to a low place in the fence at dusk one evening, securing it so the smaller dogs couldn't squeeze through, when he felt a giant fist smack him squarely in the chest. He looked around in surprise to see who'd hit him. His legs—where had they gone? Soft meadow grasses pillowed his cheek as he folded gently onto the ground. The gray twilight faded to black.

Marilyn

Siobhan was making the most ungodly

racket. I'd never heard such a wailing, keening howl. What on Earth? I stepped out on the porch and looked around in the gathering dusk. Couldn't see anything. Went back in the house to tend the chicken I was frying for supper -- Jim's favorite. But the howling continued, and then the other dogs took it up. I turned the burner off under the skillet and followed the wails toward the creek, the last spot I'd seen Jim working on the fence.

I saw a low, long shape on the ground and over it stood Siobhan, her muzzle pointed straight up as she howled. Had she killed a deer? Surely not, she was a pet, not a hunter. The primal sound sent a frisson of fear down my spine, and somehow I knew before I knew. I ran.

"Siobhan! Hush, girl. Let me see. Oh, Jim, my God!"

I knelt beside him, feeling his neck for a pulse. Faintly, faintly, I felt a flutter under my fingertips. He was alive. I reached for my cell phone in the pocket of my jeans, remembering then that it was on the charger back in the kitchen.

"Jim, hang on. Don't you dare leave! I'll be right back with help."

Siobhan resumed her stance over Jim's body, and I ran as fast as I could back to the house. It felt like one of those awful dreams where the harder you try to run, the slower your feet go. The gentle incline up to the porch had me gasping so that I could hardly get the words out to the 911 operator. I managed to give the address and country-style directions -- left at the farm stand, then two more miles and on the right. Then I grabbed a warm throw from the back of the sofa and ran back to Jim. Siobhan and I huddled there close beside him, and we never stopped begging him to hang on, each in our own way, until I heard the sirens approaching. Then I ran to the road to flag down the ambulance.

"Jump in," said one of the EMTs, holding open his door, and I did.

We bumped over the meadow to Jim's side, and when the headlights picked out his body on the ground, the medics leaped from the ambulance with their big black bags and a stretcher. But Siobhan didn't know about rescue workers; she only knew her master was down and strangers were approaching too fast with threatening objects in their hands. Baring her teeth in a snarl, probably the first one of her life, she crouched over Jim. It was a stand-off, and it was my job to safeguard them both -- Jim *and* his dearly-loved dog.

Everything in me screamed to hurry, hurry, but I took a deep breath, relaxed my shoulders and moved toward Siobhan slowly. I spoke to her softly but with authority, as Jim had taught me.

"Come on, girl, let us help. Shhh, shhh, come away now, Siobhan, we've got this, come away, good dog, be a good dog."

She lowered her head, stepped over Jim's body and came to my side. I put my hand on her neck, feeling us both shaking with anxiety. The medics wasted no time loading Jim onto the stretcher and taking off for the hospital in town, sirens blaring. It wasn't lost on me that this was the second time in my life that I'd watched someone I loved carried off on a stretcher. Someone I love.

CHAPTER FIFTEEN

Bella

"Oh my God!"

One of the band members looked up in alarm as the bus trundled through the flat dry plains of Texas. The others, including Darren, were dozing in that road-induced coma that comes with long rides. Comfortable in sweats, my hair pulled back in a messy pony tail, I sat cross legged on the sofa, fiddling with my laptop. Just for fun, I Googled my name to see if any new reviews had been posted online.

The first site that came up was Snitch, which billed itself as the purveyor of down-and-dirty gossip about country music stars. I'd seen some pretty raunchy items on Snitch, and was always glad my star was too small to warrant such exposure.

But today, to my horror, there I was -- and I mean all of me -- naked and passionately entwined with none other than Miguel. The phrase that jumped through my mind, probably from a television cop show, was *in flagrante delicto.*

"What this hot young country newcomer does in her spare time," the caption read. "Film at eleven!"

I jumped up, but blackness creeping in from the sides of my vision sat me down again as bile rose in my throat. I must have made a sound because Darren was at my side in an instant, pushing my head down between my knees. I felt his warm hand on my back anchoring me to the world. When I straightened up, I saw that he was looking at the picture on the screen.

"Oh, Darren," I said.

"Now just relax, Bella. Just relax. It's nothing. Nobody's dead, nobody's hurt, it's just a photo," he said, his voice sounding tinny.

"But, my God! When did he-- I mean, to post something like that, where everyone can see it. He must really hate me."

Forcing myself to look again at the photograph, I recognized my old apartment bedroom. I could tell from the angle exactly where Miguel had hidden the camera - on top of a tall armoire, hidden among storage baskets, a place I seldom even dusted. How long had it been there? When did Miguel plant it, and with what foreknowledge of how he'd use the pictures?

"She just saw something that upset her," Darren explained to the band members. Roused by the stress in our voices, they were looking at us curiously. "Nothing much, really, nothing to worry about," he added.

The guys went back to their naps or computer solitaire or idle guitar strumming. They'd seen it all, their postures said, but somehow I doubted if they'd look so nonchalant if they'd seen *this.*

I turned to Darren. "I'm so sorry."

"Hey, no big thing," he said, his face white with shock. "We'll get Larry on it right away, get an order or something to make Snitch take the photo down."

"Once it's on the Internet, does it ever really go away?" I asked. "And besides, if there is one photo, you can bet there will be more. Miguel is nothing if not an efficient stalker."

"Bella, this only damages you if you let it," Darren said.

I could tell he was thinking hard, putting his own feelings aside as he struggled to address this threat.

"Ignore it," he continued. "If you're questioned by the press or a fan, say you're disappointed that someone you cared about would cheapen your former relationship. Then don't say any more about it."

I stared at him in amazement. He was hurt, I could see that, and yet his mind was clicking away, finding solutions, minimizing damage, reassuring *me*, the source of his pain. But he wasn't meeting my eyes.

"Darren, I'm so sorry," I said again, around the big lump in my throat. "Even though you knew that Miguel and I lived together, it's not a pretty sight to see your girlfriend in that... situation."

"My girlfriend? You've never called yourself that before. Is that how you think of us, as a couple?"

"Well, yes. Don't you?"

"I didn't quite dare. I thought maybe I was

just useful to you."

"And you are, but you're more than useful. You're my rock, Darren. I can count on you to tell me the truth and to pull me up short when I get carried away. I couldn't possibly have gotten everything ready to go on this tour without your help."

It sounded lame and all about me, but I lacked the energy to reassure Darren more convincingly. I wished he'd stop trying to pin me down.

Star

The Department of Family and Children's Services was a tough nut to crack. The case worker assigned to the children seemed sympathetic when she heard the story of our relationship with the Kaufmans. I suppose it helped that the kids lit up whenever we were allowed to visit, with Joy attaching herself to Rowan, wrapping her legs and arms around him like a little orangutan.

But DFCS was a battleship on the seas of life, and it could not be hurried or turned on a dime. With all deliberate speed, we dotted the i's and crossed the t's.

We had medical exams to prove we were healthy. We were screened by the Child Protective Services and the National Sex Offenders Registry. Our names were run through the data bases of Pardons and Parole and the Department of Corrections. We attended information sessions and parenting lessons. We had home assessment visits. And we waited.

Each time we saw the kids, they looked less like themselves and more like wards of the state. Julia stopped brushing her hair and everyone else's. The boys took on a pugnacious loudness that Jane would have swatted down in a minute. Jennie was wetting the bed again; little Joy had purple circles under her eyes as dark as bruises.

"Please!" Rowan begged the social worker. "Please, just let us take them home. It's cheaper for the state, right? And they know us and want to come. Please get these kids out of the system before they are totally demoralized."

"I know, Mr. Greene, I'm doing my best," she replied. "I'm trying to get a court date for a judge to release the kids to you. The system is backed up; there's nothing I can do about that."

But Rowan thought there was something he could do. He played handball with an attorney who practiced family law. Although they had a strict rule that real life was not to invade the handball court, he broke that rule and begged for help.

"Okay, okay," his hapless partner finally conceded, "let me make a couple of calls."

It took a while. The most cooperative judge was out of town and we thought it wise to wait for him to get back. Then we waited some more while his clerk found a spot on his calendar. Finally, the day came, our day in court.

It was like getting ready for a first date. Rowan changed his tie three times and I had outfits strewn across the bed, tried and rejected. Finally, we were ready and checked each other out for that look of solid responsibility that we hoped would impress the judge.

There's something in a court room that lands upon you the full weight of the law. Maybe it's the echo of lives saved or ruined, the tears and fears of both the innocent and the guilty. It permeated the atmosphere.

The children were led into the room by their social worker, who tried and failed to stop Joy from running to Rowan. He scooped her up, and she buried her face in his shoulder. Thus we went forward to face the judge, who smiled down at us with genuine kindness in his eyes.

"I understand you want to be foster parents," he began.

"We do, your honor, as a step toward adoption," I said. "These children seem like our own already. We hope to legally become a family as soon as possible."

"I have your case file before me," the judge said, "and I see that you have completed all the necessary screenings and orientations and that you have visited the children on every occasion allowed. The children's social worker has written you a glowing recommendation. But I wonder; do you fully realize the magnitude of the step you are about to take?"

"We do, your honor," we said together

The judge spoke directly to the kids.

"You children have suffered a terrible loss in your lives, and my job is to make sure you get the best care possible. I am about to turn you over to the Greenes. If there is any reason why you don't want me to do that, you must tell me now," he said.

"We want to live with them," Julia said.

"Boys?"

"Yes, sir!"

"I wanna go to their house," Jennifer said around her thumb, which she'd started sucking again at about the same time she reverted to wetting the bed.

"I guess I don't need to ask the little one," the judge said, smiling at the death grip Joy had on Rowan.

There were a few more questions and some paperwork to complete, and then he signed the order and the Kaufman kids were officially in our care. We went out to the new van purchased just for them, with room for two car seats for the little girls, plenty of room in the back seat for Julia and the boys, and Rowan and me -- Mom and Dad? -- up front. We went home.

The kids ran through the house excitedly, joyfully reclaiming each remembered place. They discovered their bedrooms and called to each other to "come and see, come and see." Then Rowan sat them down for what he effortlessly called a family meeting. I was amazed. What did he know about family meetings?

"Kids," he said, "you know that the foster part is just for now. We hope to legally adopt you as soon as possible, if you want that, too."

They all nodded solemnly, even the baby.

"I know Mom would be glad," Julia said. "She'd want us all to stay together."

I heard the reservation in her voice and thought I understood it. She'd endured the unendurable and survived by pretending to a maturity there was no way she could yet possess. Was she now expected to abandon her mother's memory for a new family? Her dignity and composure wrung my heart and I felt very close to her. I groped for the right words.

"We'll never forget your Mom," I said. "We'll celebrate her birthday every year and talk about her a lot. I'm new to this job of being a mom, and I'm sure I'll make mistakes, but I love all of you, and I promise I'll do my best. I hope eventually I'll have my own place in your hearts, but your Mom will always have first place."

I had a quick flash forward: doors slamming to the tune of, "You're not my *real* mother!" which proved to be prescient. But I also saw a family: celebrating victories and weathering defeats, quarreling and reconciling, making good decisions and bad, retreating and advancing in the dance of life, weaving bright ribbons of love and loyalty into ties that would bind us together forever. And that proved to be prescient, too.

Bella

The next stop on the tour was a Texas auditorium that seemed, like everything else in the state, super-sized. The pre-show run-through was confusing and the back stage area felt like a rat-maze of narrow hallways and dressing rooms. Maybe it was just me; I was having trouble concentrating.

The guys in the band had definitely seen the

Snitch posting. I detected a subtle change in their manner. Before, they'd treated me like a little sister but now they eyed me speculatively. I felt their glances travel from my head to my toes in a kind of male inventory that made me uncomfortable.

When I stepped into the spotlight for my first number on opening night, I heard something new: wolf whistles, a few catcalls, some heckling.

"Hey, Snitch girl! Is that Snitch or Snatch?"

"Do it to me, baby!"

"Let's take some pictures! Got my camera right here."

That kind of thing. I kept on singing, but what I wanted to do was run away and hide. Darren stood behind the curtain only a few feet away from me and held me in a steady gaze. Every time I glanced at him, he nodded calmly. Somehow, that helped, and I was able to finish my set and get myself off the stage without losing what little dignity I had left.

"I don't know if I can do this." I sobbed in his arms, my stage makeup melting onto his shirt. "I feel like I've been stripped naked and paraded through the streets. I just want to go home, but I don't even have a home to go to."

"You're the same person you were before Miguel posted the photos," Darren said. "This will pass, and you'll still be the same person. And if you want a home, a permanent home base, you can have one. You've got money, remember? We've both got money."

Sometimes I actually did forget that. Breaking into the country music scene, the money didn't mean a thing. I either had the talent and drive or I didn't, and no amount of money could buy success.

I heard the LadyBugs take the stage to a thunderous ovation. I knew the group had had their own troubles with bad publicity, even a period of blackballing by some radio stations when one of them voiced an unpopular political opinion. Would that make them more sympathetic to my predicament? I opened for them at their pleasure, after all. That could change at any moment if I became a liability.

"What you've got to do now is act like a professional," Darren said. "Come on, fix your face and get changed. We're going out to dinner."

"Darren, no! I don't want to face reporters and fans right now."

"You must. If you hide, if you act ashamed, it will be like spreading blood in the water of the shark tank. You've got to tough this out. Try to look at it this way: it's publicity you couldn't buy."

Somehow that didn't help.

~*~

The tour was like a tide; it rolled on willy-nilly and we went with it. Miguel posted new pictures every couple of days, even though Larry was getting rich on legal maneuvers to prevent it. I dreaded every performance now, anticipating the crude remarks yelled out from the audience, knowing that strangers had seen me in the most intimate moments of my life. It was affecting my health. My trademark Levis and white tee-shirts hung on me and no amount of stage make-up could conceal the dark circles under my eyes. Darren was worried.

"You've got to eat and sleep, Bella," he repeated patiently every day. He'd bring my favorite foods and turn down the sheets on my bed on the bus. Sometimes I could drift off if he read to me, and we got through *Emma* and *Jane Eyre* that way. But after a couple of hours, my eyes would blink open. Then a new misery was added: I began vomiting every time I woke.

"Bella," Darren said, "I know you're doing your best and I don't want to scare you, but I'm worried. Let's work in a doctor appointment at the next stop, okay?"

I nodded mutely. Something had to give, even I could see that. Darren picked up his laptop and when we arrived at the next tour stop, I had an appointment with an internist.

We dropped off the band at the next venue to set up and do sound checks. Then, without the proper license, Darren crossed his fingers and drove the tour bus to the doctor's office, careful to lumber along in compliance with all speed limits. He parked in the farthest corner of the big parking lot, breathing a sigh of relief.

"I'll wait here for you, shall I?" he asked.

"Yes, thanks, I'd rather go in alone."

She was a motherly-looking, middle-aged woman, this doctor who didn't know or care what I did for a living. Her manner was brisk and impersonal, and the examination was thorough. She spent a long time palpating my abdomen and listening through her stethoscope. I peed in a cup and held out my arm to give blood. Then she told me to get dressed and we'd talk in her office.

"Well, Mrs. Morales," she began.

I opened my mouth to say, "It's miss," but closed it without speaking. What did it matter?

"You are basically a healthy young woman, although you're a little underweight so I'd like to see you gain a few pounds. I have patients who would kill to hear me say that."

"What's wrong with me, then? Why do I feel so rotten all the time?"

"Are you under stress?" she asked.

I laughed a little. "Yeah, I am. I am under stress."

To my horror, two large tears dropped into my lap. She pushed a tissue box toward me matter-of-factly. I could tell she'd dealt with many a weeping patient.

"Mrs. Morales, you strike me as a resourceful young woman. I strongly recommend that you find ways to reduce your stress level. It's important for your health, and at this point, if I am correct, it's even more important."

She paused, smiling at me from across her desk.

"We won't know for sure until we get the test results, and I'm no obstetrician, but I believe you may be pregnant."

After that, I didn't hear what else she said. I must have responded, I must have paid my bill and left the office. Darren was waiting in the bus and looked at me inquiringly when I climbed aboard.

"Well? What did the doctor say?"

"I'm... maybe-- She said I might be pregnant."

I had no agenda when I blurted out those words. I didn't expect Darren's face to blaze with emotion like it did. I didn't think he'd grab me into the biggest hug of my life. I never dreamed his eyes would fill with tears.

"A baby! Bella, *our* baby!"

"But... my career. I'm just getting started."

"And you don't have to quit. But are you having fun? Is it everything you dreamed it would be?"

His words stopped me cold. Was performing on tour fun? If I was being honest, no, not anymore, it was horrible. Was it my dream come true? Maybe, but dreams can turn to nightmares and this one had.

"What do *you* want?" he asked.

"I'm not sure. It would feel so wrong to stop performing, like I'm giving up on my dream when it's so close to coming true."

"You don't have to make a decision right now. We need to get those test results back and make sure you really are pregnant. Then we can think what to do next. But remember, you get to choose. If you want to continue in the music business, you can -- country music fans love the stars' families, too. If you want to stop performing for a while, maybe pick it back up later, you can do that; you're young enough for several do-overs. If you want to retire from the business, sell this bus, buy a house somewhere and be a mom, you can.

Here he paused and added with new intensity, "If you want to marry me, I would love nothing more in this world."

"But the photos, Darren. Can you ever forget seeing those images?"

"I already have."

He'd been holding me close, but now he put me at arm's length so he could look into my eyes. He spoke slowly and emotionally.

"Bella, I want to marry you and make a home for our child. But even if it means we don't get married, the most important thing is that you freely choose what you truly want. You cannot let yourself be chased out of the business by Miguel; you mustn't use the baby as an excuse to get out of an uncomfortable situation. You must not hide. Whatever you decide to do, hold your head up. It's the rest of your life"

CHAPTER SIXTEEN

Marilyn

I scrambled to my car, ready to follow the ambulance to the hospital, but first I put Siobhan into the garage. She was in such a state I was afraid she might try to find Jim herself. Then I drove faster than I'd ever driven in my life.

Jim was in a treatment room in the Emergency Department and I wasn't allowed to go to him. I paced the waiting room until finally a nurse came out and said Dr. Miller was being taken to a room in Cardiac Intensive Care.

"Will he be all right?" I asked.

"The doctor will give you more information," she said. "And you are?"

"Just a friend," I said, wishing I had a better claim.

"Do you know of any family?"

"I don't. He doesn't have children and his wife died. His office staff may know of someone to contact, but they won't be open until Monday morning and I don't know how to get in touch with any of them."

"Then I guess you're it," she said cheerfully.

"I'll tell the doctor you're here."

We huddled in the hall, the cardiologist and I. She was a ridiculously young woman with an air of calm competence that made up for her lack of years.

"Is he going to live?" I asked, too scared to be anything but blunt.

"Yes," she replied. "It was a serious heart attack, but he's in good health generally and he can make a full recovery. Oops, are you all right?"

She reached out a steadying hand. "Yes, sorry, it's such good news." I put my hand on the wall for support. Why is good news sometimes as unnerving as bad?

"Well, I expect you've had quite a day," the cardiologist continued. "You can see Dr. Miller in a minute, and that will make you feel better."

She was right. Although tubes snaked from his nose and mouth, an IV dripped fluid into his arm and monitors displayed his body's innermost secrets for all to see, I was comforted that his chest was moving reliably up and down. I said his name and he opened his eyes. They were filled with questions.

"Jim. Do you know where you are? Do you know what happened to you?"

Slight shake of the head: no.

"You're in the hospital in Centerville. You had a heart attack while you were working on the fence. But listen, Jim: you're going to be fine."

Another slight shake of the head: no.

~*~

Jim's body got better. After his release from

the hospital, he dutifully attended his rehab sessions, shuffled along on the treadmill, swallowed his pills and removed the salt shaker from the table. But something was missing, something vital. The spark that made him Jim was gone and only a dull-eyed man remained.

I kept Siobhan at my place, and Jim never even asked about his beloved dog when I drove him to rehab every other day. Making conversation was painfully difficult. I could hardly believe this was the same Jim with whom I could talk for hours.

On a day when he didn't have rehab, I took Siobhan and several carefully prepared meals and paid him an unannounced visit. Siobhan was beside herself with joy to see Jim, but he responded listlessly. The dog finally subsided, laying her head on his foot with a gusty sigh. Then we sat in silence. My efforts at conversation went thud. Finally, I'd had enough.

"Okay, Jim, what's up?" I demanded.

"Nothing. Sorry. Just tired."

"You're more than tired. Tell me what's bothering you."

"I had a heart attack!" he shouted, tears springing into his eyes.

He'd never raised his voice to me before, and I blinked in surprise. Yes, I'd been told by the rehab specialist to expect this, that heart attack victims are often angry and emotional. Still, it was a shock. I spoke slowly, as I'd spoken to Siobhan that awful night.

"You did. But now you're better. Soon you can pick up your life again and get back to what you enjoy."

"I think I'm pretty well finished, Marilyn. Not much I can do now but sit in a chair and wait to die."

"Why, Jim Miller. What a load of crap! Did that heart attack affect your brain? You're not the first person to have one, you know. People get better; they get *well.* And by God, so will you. I won't have you moping around feeling sorry for yourself. It's not like you and I simply won't allow it. You've got your practice and for that matter, you've got some big ideas for my place. Now that you've got me all enthused, don't think you're going to dump all that work on me while you slink around like a sick cat. Three more dogs showed up this past week, and you know damn well I can't take care of them by myself. So you just get over your little pity party, mister, because you've got work to do."

I stopped, out of breath, cheeks burning. Who did I think I was, to throw a fit and yell at this poor, sick man? But his mouth was twitching. He was smiling. Then he was chuckling. Then we were both laughing, and he became Jim again. The self-pity was gone and it never returned.

The next week, he called and asked me to come and get him. He wasn't allowed to drive yet, but he said, "I want to take a look at the plans for our dog sanctuary. I've got a few ideas for changes. We need to get cracking on that."

Our; we. I couldn't get into the car fast enough.

~*~

We did need to get cracking. Progress had been delayed by Jim's illness and now by his slower pace as he recovered. The first step was rezoning the property and that involved a neighborhood meeting called by the county commissioner for our district. Jim was well enough to be at my side as I nervously stood behind the podium and attempted to explain what I wanted to do.

"Since I moved out here, there's been a steady stream of dogs put out of their owners' cars at the foot of my driveway. These poor animals are scared and lost. My dog, Sam, brings them up to the house and I just can't turn them away. Dr. Miller, whom many of you already know, suggested that I create a no-kill sanctuary for them, with appropriate buildings and community volunteers to help out."

My audience looked unmoved. A man stood up in the back of the room.

"What about the noise and the smells?" he asked. "I don't want to hear dogs yapping every hour of the day and night."

"And I don't want my neighborhood to become known as the dumping grounds for unwanted animals," a woman added.

"Will there be a limit on how many dogs you can keep at your place?" another asked.

All good questions, but I felt myself getting panicky at the hostility I sensed behind them. Jim came to my rescue, stepping smoothly to my side.

"Hi, I'm Dr. Jim Miller. I will serve as Medical Director of Miss Simmons' sanctuary. We've brought our business plan for you to study. It outlines the number of dogs we will house, our plans for their care and our mission to find them homes. I can assure you that the facilities will be kept spotlessly clean, so there will be no odor. As for the noise, our goal is to have quiet, contented dogs. They will not be confined to cages 24/7, which leads to a lot of bored, nervous barking, but will have the run of large outdoor areas and plenty of human contact. My cell phone number is listed in the plan, and I invite you to call me at any time of the day or night that you are disturbed by barking."

A teenage girl raised her hand tentatively. "What will the volunteers do?" she asked.

"Volunteers will have several jobs to choose from," Jim said, smiling at her. "They'll clean cages, walk, groom and socialize the dogs, answer the phone in the office, work online with adoption organizations, and help with meal times. Are you interested in volunteering?"

She nodded, whispering urgently to a woman who was obviously her mother. "Who's going to pay for all this?" someone called out.

"I am," I said. "I've endowed the sanctuary with a sum that my accountants tell me will fund it for many years. The financial arrangements are on page three of the business plan. Does everyone have a copy of the plan?"

Jim walked the aisles, handing out plans to those who hadn't picked them up at the door. I spoke again.

"I know change can be disruptive to an established neighborhood. I've only lived among you for a short time, but I've come to love the privacy and rural atmosphere. I wouldn't want to endanger that for myself or any of us. But my heart is hurt by the plight of these poor dogs. Maybe the owners that dump them think they are being kinder than if they took them to a shelter, but I see the results. Dogs that have been family pets are suddenly on their own in a strange place. They don't know how to take care of themselves; they are pets, not hunters. Some of them bear marks of abuse and are afraid of people. My dog, Sam, coaxes them to come to the house."

I stopped, unable to continue around the lump in my throat. Jim gave my shoulder a reassuring squeeze as he took over.

"Some of you may know that I recently had a heart attack," he said. "It really made me realize how precious every day is. I thought a lot about how I want to spend the rest of my time in this world, and I realized that I want to spend it rescuing dogs. Their lives are precious to them, just as mine is to me, and I think they deserve a chance. I hope you will help. Marilyn and I can't do it without you."

I felt the mood of the room change as people shifted in their chairs and whispered comments to their neighbors. For the first time, they were on our side. The commissioner again took charge of the meeting.

"We've been provided with a great deal of information," she said. "I will welcome your input, either in person, by phone, or by e-mail. It will be taken into account by the zoning board."

We talked with folks after the meeting -- what Jim called pressing the flesh -- and I thought most of their questions and comments seemed interested and friendly. Several said they might see about volunteering if our project ever got off the ground. Little Mike and his parents were there and he gave me a reassuring thumbs-up. I heard him say, "I help out on the grounds."

We swung between hope and despair as we waited for the next meeting of the county zoning board. When it came, Jim and I were in the audience early so we could get front row seats. We were armed with copies of our business plan and ready to answer questions. To our surprise, it was over in a minute.

"I move... I second... carried."

Our zoning application was approved.

"It seemed simple only because we put so much work into the application," Jim said afterward, while we were having a celebratory drink. "We addressed every question and contingency before they had a chance to ask. Now we can really get going."

He beamed at me and I could feel an answering smile stretching across my face. I cared about the dogs and I was excited about the project. But the best thing was sharing it with Jim.

Darren

I failed Bella when Miguel found a way past my protective barrier, that was obvious, but we never once thought he'd attack through the Internet. When those photos came up on the Snitch site -- well, who could've see *that* coming? Bella was devastated, and I'll confess I was, too, although I hope I hid it from her. I had some long, strong talks with myself: *you knew they were together, you knew they had sex, so this is not an earth-shattering revelation. You are with her now, not Miguel. She's the same girl she was before the pictures appeared; you loved her then, you still love her now.*

Gradually, reason replaced revulsion and I came to grips with it. I'm not saying it was easy, but as Woody Allen famously said, the heart wants what the heart wants, and my heart wanted Bella.

Watching her struggle through the shows was as hard as anything I've ever had to do. I wanted to go out into the audience and slug the creeps who were yelling ugly things. I wanted to sweep Bella off the stage and carry her away. I wanted to find Miguel and put a bullet in his brain.

I did none of it. What I did do was remain calm and project that calmness to Bella. Sometimes I marveled that the secret-vodka-drinking Mama's boy had become someone's rock, but I knew I was Bella's.

When I became alarmed enough about her health to persuade her into a doctor visit, I was blind-sided by the news she brought back. On reflection, I seem to have been rather clueless all the way around. But when she said "pregnant," everything fell into place in my head. Of course! We were going to have a baby! We would be a family. My Mom would love being a grandmother. I would love being a daddy. Bella would be a terrific mother... with a mental shake, I pulled myself together.

Give me the right words, I prayed. *Let me say*

the right words now, if I never say them again in my life.

Bella

Darren said just the right words. He gave me the freedom to choose and that carried me from blind panic to rational thought. What did I really want?

Performing was my lifelong dream and, while I proved I could make it as a professional singer, it wasn't the grand fulfillment I thought it would be. The initial exhilaration of singing before an audience was replaced with exhaustion. I had to admit to myself that traveling, having no home except the bus, made me feel rootless and sad. Miguel's photos added a layer of shame. Even before I found out I was pregnant, I'd been trying to stifle serious second thoughts. I didn't want to be a quitter. Early success had come easily; now I had to decide if I had the will to reach the top.

Neither Darren nor I ever spoke the word "abortion." That was one option that didn't seem to be on the table for either of us. From some place I didn't know I had, came a swell of maternal feeling. No way was I going to miss out on having this baby. I wanted a home, my own family.

"But what about the band?" I asked Darren. "It's so unfair to just leave them in the lurch. They're doing a great job for me."

"Let's just talk to them about it. You're already paying them twice the going rate. Maybe they've saved up."

We looked at each other doubtfully. The band members didn't seem like the saving-up kind, nor did what we saw of their lifestyles hint at this. We found a moment to talk to Boyd alone.

"I have news," I began.

"You're leaving the tour," Boyd finished for me.

"How did you know?"

"It don't take a genius to see that you ain't having fun anymore. And with your money, why should you keep on being miserable?"

"Do you hate me for it, Boyd? Will the other guys hate me?"

"Not for a minute. We've gotten to be a pretty decent band while backing you up. I ain't the singer you are, but I think I could handle lead vocals if we change the focus a little, go in for an edgier sound. We'd like to talk to the LadyBugs about staying on as their opening act -- without you. Would you mind?"

"Of course not. Nothing would make me happier. If you think it would help, I'll put in a good word for you, although I may not be their favorite person right now."

But the LadyBugs were supportive. They'd seen the Snitch items and they'd watched me slowly fade away in the spotlight I'd craved. Combined with the news of my pregnancy, they said it made sense to take a breather. That was tactful; none of us knew whether I was taking a breather or retiring after a very brief career. They were willing to give Bowie County a trial and with that settled, the final pieces dropped into place.

There was the matter of the bus. Buying it

now seemed like the stupidest decision I'd ever made. What was I going to do with a half-million dollar tour bus in the middle of Texas? I suggested to Boyd that I rent it to him and the band for a dollar a year, but he just laughed.

"Darlin', do you know how many miles this bus gets to a gallon of gas? About six! No thanks, that's a mighty kind offer, but me and the boys will get us a bus more in keeping with our billfolds. Shoot, I've toured in a 1998 Dodge Dart before. All this luxury is nice, but it ain't necessary for us. We're used to roughing it. You just get Big Bertha here back to Nashville and sell her if you're sure you won't need her."

It meant flying a bus driver out from Nashville and paying him to drive the bus back to the broker. Free of our hulking home on wheels and feeling like turtles suddenly free of their shells, we caught a plane back. We went home. But we had a problem: we had no home to go to.

I booked a suite for us at the Ritz. Darren's mother lobbied hard for him to move back in with her. She said that what she referred to as "Bella's failure" was punishment for our living in sin. Pulling out all the stops, she added heart palpitations, shame before the neighbors and Bible verses about the wages of sin. But this time, Darren faced her down.

He told me about it. "I said, 'Bella didn't fail. She went after her dream and it turned out to be different than she expected, so she made a new plan. And that plan includes your grandbaby. I think you will want to see that baby, Mom.' She got the hint."

Then we started house-hunting, with the implicit understanding that we were looking for a home we'd share, a home for our family.

There were no more items in Snitch. Nobody cared about my private life anymore. Miguel lost a good source of income.

I didn't know until much later that Darren didn't let the matter rest there. At the time, his first priority was to make sure my pregnancy was as worry-free as possible, so he didn't tell me until our baby was here that he'd reported Miguel to the police, and a warrant had been issued for his arrest.

The pictures Miguel posted of me were considered revenge porn, and in our state such postings are illegal. Knowing this crime might fall rather far down the list of priorities for the local cops, Darren hired a private firm to track Miguel down. They found him in El Paso, about to cross the border into Mexico. The local authorities arrested him; he's been in jail ever since, unable to make bail, awaiting trial.

That trial is coming up, and I will face Miguel for the last time from the witness stand when I testify against him.

CHAPTER SEVENTEEN

Scott

The older kids came every third weekend, just as the court ordered. A nanny service sent someone to do the chores, and I played Fun Dad: taking the kids out on the boat, playing in the pool with them, letting them eat junk food and stay up too late. When they got tired and cranky I handed them over to the nanny du jour. We seldom had the same person twice.

Katie and Danny whined a lot. It was like water dripping on stone, that constant sniveling and wailing. Jessie always managed them when they got like that. I didn't know what else to do but turn them over to the nanny. It took all the will power I could muster not to drink until they were tucked into bed.

When I was on my own, I devoted my evenings to bar-hopping. I got to be a regular at a couple of places and people there called me by name, just like on Cheers. But it took more and more booze to get me buzzed and longer and longer to recover the next day. I didn't know it, but I was in the market for something new when I met Chet.

"Hey."

I looked at the guy sitting next to me at the bar. Never saw him before. I wasn't in a good mood and I looked away without answering.

He was there again the following night and this time I'd had a few and felt more sociable. We fell into a boozy conversation. He seemed, just then, like the funniest guy in the place -- maybe in the whole world. We went on to the next bar together and then to another one. I picked up all the tabs. I needed a friend, you know? Somebody who didn't judge me, who was good for some laughs, for Chrissake. From then on, I looked for him every night and he was usually there.

I noticed that Chet didn't drink as much as I did, but made several trips to the bathroom. When he came back, he was always cool, full of easy laughter and ideas. I asked him once what he did in the bathroom, and he said, "No worries, dude, just a little H. You ought to try it sometime. It's quicker than booze and so much better."

The first time I saw him inject himself, it made me sick. He couldn't find a vein in his arm so he stuck the needle between his toes. It looked disgusting, but he was one mellow fellow a couple of minutes later.

I was tempted. Drinking wasn't doing much for me anymore and the hangovers were increasingly debilitating. The black dog was always there waiting, even when I drank myself to oblivion. Especially then. Maybe I needed something different; maybe I'd try it just to see what it was like. Chet fixed me up.

The very first time I used heroin, I loved it. I

loved the sweeping rush of good feeling, the heightened senses, the flood of sensation followed by complete relaxation, being one with the universe or whatever. It just felt great. And hey, I could afford it. I wouldn't ever be one of those junkies selling his blood to buy the next hit. I could afford clean needles and high quality smack, probably no more harmful than tobacco or alcohol. I could always stop if it was getting out of hand. Right?

In a very short time, I developed a very expensive habit that Chet just happened to be able to fill. I bought enough to share with him. He took to coming out to the house in the late afternoons and we'd just hang around at home, shooting up. It was easier than bar-hopping and we weren't that interested in drinking or picking up women any more. The black dog was gone, maybe for good.

I knew I'd better not use when the kids were with me. But sometimes I needed a little hit to get straight, just enough so I could take care of them. Being high gave me more patience, like a good daddy. So it was a positive thing, and I could handle it without overdoing it.

~*~

The kids are with me again, so it must be a weekend. We're out by the pool, and I'm a little high. The new nanny sizes up the situation in a minute and says she wants a hit, too. She doesn't have to mention it's a bribe to keep her quiet. I'm not so far gone that I can't figure that out. Well, why not? We can manage just fine between the two of us, even a little bit high.

The kids are in the pool, and I'm laughing and laughing at Danny's attempts at swimming. Little guy can really move those arms and legs. I fish him out and he's playing with a toy of some kind right there beside me. My head keeps dropping forward but I jerk awake. Nanny is zoned out, smiling up at the sun. But I know it's important to watch the kids around the pool, very important. So I'm watching....

Then Katie's screaming so loud, God, she's so loud, and the nanny is screaming, too and Danny is floating quietly in the pool. Nanny dives in the pool with a big splash. I try to get up, try to wake up, but maybe I doze back off for a minute or two, no more than that.

Then somebody's shaking me. I try to open my eyes but I can't focus. There are two of everything, which strikes me funny. Maybe it's not good to laugh right now when everybody's so serious but I can't help it. Two guys in uniforms are standing over Danny and one of them keeps pushing on his chest, pushing and pushing.

"Hey, man, leave the little dude alone," I thought, or maybe I said it.

The man doing the pushing doesn't even look at me, but the other one says, "Shut up, you worthless piece of junkie shit, you let your little boy drown."

What? Drown? No, he could swim, I saw him swim. Did they say... Is he dead? No, no, Danny can't be dead. My fault, my fault!

Then Jessie's angry face looms over me, blotting out the sky, her mouth wide open as she screams. I can't deal with it; I'm crying. She's such a bitch, so mean. Not sure what happened. Something about Danny? Better to escape into sleep. When I wake again, it's quiet, thank God. Nobody's around, not even Chet.

Let's see, where are the kids? Did something bad happen? My mind skitters up to and away from the word "drowned." No, no, no.

I see the black dog's eyes gleaming in the corner. I need more stuff, need not to see him anymore, need to be able to think. I have a stash. I'll shoot up a little bit more, just enough to take the edge off... just enough....

Marilyn

"We need a name," I said. "We can't just go on calling it 'my house."

"I've been thinking about that," Jim said. "How about Per-Simmons Sanctuary? You know: Per-hyphen-Simmons. It's a play on your name and on the big persimmon tree down by the creek. Persimmon fruit is sour when it's young, but sweet when it's ripe, just like a good woman. Just like you."

"Okay, okay! I can't always tell when you're kidding," I said, "but actually -- I kinda like it if we leave out the hyphen."

At first, Persimmon Sanctuary was anything but peaceful. The next few months of hammering and sawing were intense. I awoke to the screech of power saws and sawdust floating in the air like beige snow, drifting over my car, the porch, the window sills and even the dogs.

At Jim's suggestion, I wrote a one-page newsletter and stuck it in my neighbors' mailboxes, describing the work that was being done and inviting them to stop by and see for themselves. A surprising number of them did, and I welcomed them with homemade chocolate chip cookies and iced tea. We sat on the porch and talked above the hammering. Sam played co-hostess and bestowed her most ingratiating smiles on our visitors. People were interested in what we were doing. They all knew Little Mike and his family and seemed reassured that a neighbor was involved.

The one constant through the entire process was Jim. He came out when he finished at the clinic -- working only half days now -- to look over what had been done, bringing beautiful Siobhan along. Then he had dinner with me in the kitchen. I cooked a good, hot meal every night, experimenting with low-sodium, low-fat recipes. I loved having a man to cook for, especially this man. I made him rest on the porch after dinner. Not too many chores, not yet. He was still recovering. Just sitting and rocking with him on the porch, watching the sun set, talking about nothing much, made the whole day worthwhile.

You are too old for dreams of romance, I lectured myself sternly every night before I fell asleep. *And even if that weren't true, what would a successful professional like Dr. Jim Miller ever see in a retired municipal clerk? We're friends, at best. Maybe I'm just a means to an end because I have enough money to finance his dearest wish. Maybe we're only business partners. Whatever we are, I won't louse everything up by having silly fantasies.*

All through the construction phase, the dogs kept coming. Mostly medium-sized black or yellow dogs, the sort I'd read were universal prototypes whether in the United States or India or Africa. There were a few small, cute dogs and I knew they would quickly be adopted. The big dogs would take longer, but I was determined they would all find homes. Altogether, I counted twenty-two already in residence on the morning of our official opening.

Jim

Finally, it was finished. The buildings were solidly constructed and contained everything Jim needed to medically care for the dogs they sheltered. Volunteers were signed up and scheduled. Dogs, there were plenty of and they kept on coming. The first big push would be finding homes for the ones in residence to make room for more.

Jim spent as much time at Persimmon Sanctuary as possible and wished for longer days and greater endurance. He saw that Marilyn co-existed with the noise and dust and set-backs of construction with good humor and patience. A couple of times he found her wearing a nail apron as she pitched in with the crew. More often, she was in the kitchen cooking his dinner. He'd look across the yard and see the warm yellow light glowing from the window over the sink; he'd smell a pot roast or spaghetti or apple pie and his stomach would rumble approvingly.

While they ate, they'd talk: books they'd read

-- happily, many of the same ones -- and movies and television programs, politics and religion and world events. And always, they talked about dogs. Marilyn had a convert's zeal for rescue, coming late to it as she had, but it was Jim's life's work, his passion and his joy. He returned to his dark, empty house with increasing reluctance at the end of every evening.

What would it be like, he wondered, to belong to Persimmon Sanctuary *and* to Marilyn Simmons? Was he too old to remarry? Too feeble now that he'd survived a major heart attack? Would Marilyn even entertain such an idea or would she think he just wanted a nurse for his old age? He'd come to love her generous heart, her grace under pressure and her sweet disposition, but did she love him?

They worked well together. They were great friends. What if she didn't return his feelings and the friendship was spoiled? He'd lose both a friend and a place very dear to him.

Marilyn

Jim and I surveyed the kennel, a long, low building with two rows of fifteen runs. Each had an inside room with a comfortable raised bed and stainless steel food bowls set in tip-proof racks. The outside spaces were deeply mulched and securely fenced, with shaded areas for hot days. There were two large open yards, one for big dogs and one for small, where the more socially secure canines could hang out together and take refreshing dips in plastic wading pools. The dispensary where Jim would treat his patients was as well-equipped as any vet's office. Beside it was a small command center with the computer and land-line phones, and a storeroom filled with supplies.

"I feel like God on the seventh day," Jim said, "I look at what we have created and say it is good."

Our first volunteers were due to arrive any minute. Little Mike had proved to be an asset for drawing in the teenage crowd -- apparently he was very popular -- and we had a long roster of kids, mostly girls, who wanted to work with the dogs.

But first there was the final touch: the installation of the sign. We crunched down the gravel driveway in our sensible farm boots to see workmen anchor a big wooden sign featuring a carved persimmon tree below the name. Jim reached for my hand as we arrived.

"Persimmon Sanctuary," I said. "How could I have ever imagined such a thing when I picked Sam up off the street in front of the rescue mission?"

"I worry that it's more my dream come true than yours," Jim said, "and with your money, at that."

"No, it's just a dream I didn't know I had," I said, "and as for the money, I hoped it would bring me freedom and joy, and it has."

To my amazement, Jim dropped down to one knee.

"Marilyn Simmons," he said, but his voice wobbled, and he had to stop and clear his throat. "I love you. I want to spend the rest of my life with you, right here at Persimmon Sanctuary. Will you be my wife? Will you marry me?"

"Why, Jim," I said, staring at him in

bewilderment, "you've never even kissed me."

"Let's fix that right now," he said, scrambling to his feet with some difficulty.

He did, to appreciative whistles from the workmen. All thoughts of being too old for romance flew out of my head. I couldn't speak for a moment, and Jim said later he got very nervous during that interval.

"Or do you need time to think?" he added.

I thought: about having this kind and clever man share my future instead of the lonely years I'd been envisioning. I thought about days filled with work I loved at the side of a man I loved -- and who, miraculously, loved me.

"I don't need to think about it," I said. "It sounds like heaven."

Bella

When my son was born -- my *Niño* -- I fell truly in love for the first time in my life. He was beautiful, perfect, totally absorbing. Darren was as proud as I of the little boy who already looked like him. We named him Darren III, which quickly became D3.

If only I could show him to his *abuelos*. If only my mama was here to help me with the puzzles of first-time motherhood. But to my surprise, Darren's mother stepped in. She'd treated me with a kind of wary politeness since we'd come back from Nashville and Darren had made it clear we were a couple, married or not. She disapproved of us living together and wondered aloud why we didn't go ahead and make it legal, but after Darren stood firm, she observed a discreet silence on the subject.

Then along came the baby, her only grandchild, and she was hopelessly smitten. Nothing mattered anymore except little Darren's health and happiness. She was as tender and supportive an almost-mother-in-law as she was a grandmother. I turned to her with breastfeeding problems, with urgent questions about burping and diaper rash, with concerns about this or that strange event in D3's day, and she always came through.

My spirits lifted when I heard her open our door. She'd always call out, "Yoo-hoo!" which made me laugh. Who does that? But I came to value her friendship and think of her as my ally. Darren was much like her; they were both rocks.

And so the hazy, sleep-deprived days of new motherhood passed. I felt completely content, but I knew Darren had a nagging concern that he tried to voice as infrequently as possible.

"When will you make an honest man of me?" he'd say, trying to sound light-hearted and funny. But I knew it was not a joke to him. I was still trying to figure out my reluctance to marry and I couldn't find the words to give Darren the explanation he deserved. It had something to do with that last glimpse of my parents and siblings boarding the ICE bus and disappearing from my life. Nor could I forget that I'd chosen Miguel, thought I loved him, let him into my life and my bed, and trusted him -- only to be smacked with a staggering betrayal. I had to admit that my track record with permanent relationships wasn't stellar. What Darren and I had seemed so good. Why change it? Why take a chance on messing it up?

CHAPTER EIGHTEEN

Darren

As far as I know, Bella has never looked back. We have our baby, our son Darren III, named after me and my father. Like the sun that comes up in the morning, little D3 also rises early and fills our days with warmth and joy. And we have our home, a rather stately pile of bricks and fieldstone on a bluff high above a river. We can look out our living room windows and see the rafters and hikers far below us.

My mother drops in a lot, and she and Bella have bonded over caring for D3. Bella has no family in this country, and as a new mother with breastfeeding issues, she was grateful for my Mom's wisdom and support. Who knew Mom was an expert on that? But life is full of surprises.

"How about you make an honest man out of me?" I ask Bella, for we are still not married.

She always replies, "One of these days, we'll just walk into the courthouse and find a nice judge and get married. No muss, no fuss."

I believe her, mostly. I tell myself that we have a long life ahead of us, and a whole world of possibilities.

We've gotten more involved with the scholarship foundation that Bella and I once dreamed up over coffee. Turns out our former city government co-workers have some great kids and a lot of them are pursuing higher education or trade school with the foundation's help. Star and Rowan are also involved in whatever time they can spare from their five children. We leave the administration up to the woman we hired to do that job, but we like to get to know the kids. Sometimes they get discouraged or need a little more help, and if we know them personally, we can step in.

The other night we had a party for them at our house. Marilyn and Jim came, and Jessie but not Scott. The Holmes' made it a point not to attend the same events, but then Scott wouldn't have come anyway. He showed up at nothing that involved the rest of us. I hadn't even seen him since Bella and I returned from the tour, but I'd heard he was in a bad way, involved with drugs and some bad kinds of people. Jessie was well rid of him, money or no money.

Bella got out her guitar and, without even being coaxed, sang for us. I stood watching her; slim in her jeans and white tee-shirt with her long dark hair framing her beautiful face, she was as enchanting as ever. I wondered if I'd ever see her singing under the bright lights again. The kids sat in a semi-circle around her and applauded every song enthusiastically. I remembered the night she took the Bluebird Café by storm and wondered if she had any regrets about the career she'd left behind. I was deep in thought when Star appeared at my side.

"Long before we ever won the lottery," she said, "we used to talk about what we'd do with the money. Bella said someday we'd have a foundation and she'd headline a show for it. And here we are, although maybe not exactly as we'd planned." She paused, and then asked, "Did you ever imagine the life you have now?"

"Not in my most outrageous dreams," I said. "Did you see yourself as the mother of five?"

"Not even of one," she said, laughing. "Is it a good life for you, Darren, the way things have worked out?"

I gave the question some thought. "It's not perfect. I'd like to get married, but Bella--I don't know, maybe she just doesn't want the commitment. She and D3 are my life and I'd like the security of marriage. Isn't that usually the woman's line? But, other than that, yes, life is good."

My phone chose that moment to vibrate and glancing at it, I saw that the caller was Jessie. But Jessie was standing across the room from me, so it couldn't be her. Curious, I excused myself, left the room and answered.

"Darren, this is Jessie's father. I'm calling on her phone because she left it behind and it has your number programmed into it."

"Yes, sir. What can I do for you? Do you need to talk to Jessie?"

"Not right now. I need to talk to you first." I heard him take a deep breath. "The police were just here. Scott is dead. The cleaning lady found him when she came to work this morning. She told the police he had a needle in his arm."

"My God. That poor bastard. I heard he was doing drugs."

"Jessie needs to come home," her father continued, "but I don't want her to drive herself. I don't want her to hear this on the car radio."

"Of course not. Don't worry, I'll take care of Jessie. I'll break the news about Scott and bring her home."

Once again, I slipped into my role as Darren, the rock. I shepherded Jessie into a room far from the festivities.

"Jessie, I have something bad to tell you. It's about Scott."

"What's he done now?"

"He's-- he's passed away. He's dead."

She looked at me incredulously, her brow furrowed as she tried to take it in.

"Dead? I know he was using some heavy drugs because he almost let Danny drown the last time he had the kids at his house. He was so out of it, I'm not sure that what happened even registered with him. The nanny was using, too, but she still had enough awareness to pull Danny out of the water, dial 911 and work on him until the paramedics arrived. Scott was asleep again, or in some kind of drug la-la land when I got the kids out of there. Needless to say, they won't ever go back..." she stopped as the realization hit her. "Are they sure he's dead? Can that be true?"

"That's what your Dad said, and he asked me to bring you home. I'm sorry, Jessie. I know this is tough."

"What a stupid, stupid waste! I can't even cry

about it. He was my first love and the father of my children, but he'd become – I don't even know who he was. He had such opportunities before him, with all that money. He could have been anything, done anything. He chose heroin instead; he chose death and now my kids will grow up without knowing their father."

She crossed the room to the bank of windows overlooking the dark garden and stood there silently for a few moments. Then I saw her square her shoulders and lift her head. She turned back to me, eyes still dry, face set in lines of sadness.

"I need to be with my kids, Darren."

I took her home.

CHAPTER NINETEEN

The Wedding

Marilyn and Jim mingled with their guests under the big persimmon tree by the stream. Decked out in fresh lime-green leaves, the tree spread its branches like a blessing over the people below. Spring sunshine laid a warm hand over the meadow, releasing the scent of wild roses along the stream bank.

Marilyn wore a dress of pale peach lace and carried a handful of white peonies she'd picked that morning, their stems wrapped in a damp lace handkerchief. Jim was resplendent in an old-fashioned white dinner jacket with a red rose pinned to the lapel. They joked that they looked like the bride and groom on top of the cake, for this was their wedding day.

Jessie shifted the baby from one shoulder to the other. Morris was a chunk, but she didn't want to risk waking him by putting him back in his pram. Katie and Daniel stood quietly at her side, lulled by sunshine and serenity. The children hadn't had much peace in their lives lately and they soaked it in.

She saw, with a mental shrug, that Danny's

white sailor suit was already grass-stained at the knees. He had recovered from his near-drowning with nothing worse to show for it than an ear infection and was so young that the scary memory was already receding in his mind. Jessie wished it would recede in hers.

Katie was angelic in a long white eyelet dress, with a circle of roses in her curls. She'd begged to be a flower girl and was given a little wicker basket full of petals, but at the last minute felt too shy to leave her mother's side.

"No problem," Marilyn had said, giving Katie a hug. "You can toss those flowers whenever you feel like it."

Katie immediately upended the basket and kicked her feet in the little mound of petals.

"Oh, Marilyn, I'm sorry," Jessie began, but Marilyn thought it was funny.

"She's three," Marilyn said, "and that's all she needs to be."

Jessie's thoughts were never far from Scott since his death. Her emotions ran a loop from rage to regret to sorrow and back again. She retained no illusions about the kind of man he'd been. If he were alive, if they had still been married, she knew he'd never have attended this simple al fresco wedding with her.

"What do I care if two old fools decide to get married?"

She could hear him say it. But *she* cared. She was warmed by Marilyn's happiness, vicariously thrilled by the unexpected second act in her life. She thought maybe someday it could happen to her. It was hard to believe.

Bella and Darren walked through the meadow arm in arm. Bella was radiant in a long blue dress, her dark hair twisted up under a big hat. Darren wore tiny D3 like a medal in a baby-sling across his chest. They looked like the picture of a happy young family, but Darren's mind was troubled. Why couldn't this be *his* wedding day?

Be happy with what you've got, you big clod. You have Bella even if you don't have a piece of paper making it legal. You have D3, the son who will carry on your name, a home full of love, plenty of money, and everybody's healthy. We're young. Our whole lives are ahead of us. Enjoy this moment. Someday it will be us getting married.

His inner pep-talk worked. He felt a surge of well-being and happiness as he stood in the sunlight waiting for Jim and Marilyn to take their vows.

Rowan and Star were there, surrounded by all five children. When she'd called to invite them to the wedding, Marilyn said very definitely that children were welcome.

"But what if Joy cries?" Star asked.

"Then we'll comfort her," Marilyn replied simply.

Star had spent some time and effort on her kids. The little girls preened in pretty summer dresses and white sandals, their hair plaited with matching ribbons. The boys wore starched white shirts already wilting under pressure, stiff new trousers and polished shoes. They tugged at their collars and gazed longingly at the stream. Baby Joy, with sleepy eyes and a thumb in her mouth, nestled in Rowan's arms.

Larry Bickler and his date stood in the shade. The two young men, in their ice-cream suits and pastel ties, looked as though they had stepped straight from the pages of a Gentlemen's Quarterly spread on what to wear to a summer wedding. Larry was beaming as proudly as a father, although the nuptial couple was old enough to be his parents. As legal advisor to all five lottery winners, he'd walked a long road with them. He felt he'd matured professionally in their service, and in the process they'd become his friends.

Except for Scott. Scott's death was a horror story, but to Larry, not entirely surprising. His money had simply turned his demons loose. Settling his estate was the last legal act Larry would perform for him. There was a will, of course. Larry had seen to that as part of estate planning, but Scott had never gotten around to signing it. Fortunately, state law dictated that his entire estate be divided among his three children, to be held in trust until they came of age. Larry worried about the effect of such affluence on the kids, but Jessie had her head screwed on straight and he'd bet on her being able to instill common sense in her children to counterbalance the dollar signs. He nudged his companion and winked as the string quartet ensconced under the persimmon tree sent Pachelbel's Canon in D wafting across the sunlit meadow. "Here we go," he whispered.

Marilyn and Jim clasped hands and walked serenely toward the bank of flowers where the minister waited. Arriving at the improvised altar of peonies, roses, ferns and lilies, they discreetly snapped their fingers. Instantly, scruffy Sam and beautiful Siobhan came to them. Sam placed one dusty paw firmly on the toe of Marilyn's peach linen shoe and smiled up at her. Marilyn smiled back and reached down to smooth her head. The bridal party was ready.

"Dearly beloved, we are gathered together...."

Jessie's eyes stung with unexpected tears. She remembered those words from her own wedding day. How could it all have gone so utterly wrong? Scott was dead and she stood alone with three little children and some bad memories.

"Do you, Marilyn, take this man... Do you, James, take this woman...."

Star felt Rowan's arm around her, warm and solid. The children watched the ceremony with wide eyes, impressed by the solemnity of the occasion. She wondered if they were remembering their mother and regretting their father. There was so much to regret, so much to overcome. And yet, there is always this ceremony, she thought, and these ancient words to make it all possible again.

"In sickness and in health, for richer or for poorer...."

Bella's hand slipped into Darren's and squeezed. When he glanced down, he saw her eyes swimming with tears. Enigmatic as always, Bella gave him a watery smile and turned her attention back to the ceremony. He decided to take it as a good sign that her heart was touched by their friends' marriage. Maybe next time these words would be spoken over them.

"By the authority vested in me, I now pronounce you...."

Jim and Marilyn exchanged a kiss before they turned to their friends and were introduced as Mr. and Mrs. James Miller. They were engulfed in hugs and congratulations.

At that moment, an improvised loudspeaker hidden in the persimmon's branches blared, "Who let the dogs out? Woof, woof-woof woof-woof." Little Mike and his harem of female kennel volunteers, delighted with their practical joke and sure of an appreciative audience, swung wide the kennel gates, and all the boarding dogs surged into the meadow. Children ran to meet them and they formed a scrum of giggles, shrieks and wagging tails.

Bella found herself beside Star, both of them laughing at a spectacle that summed up Marilyn and Jim to perfection. Heedless of their wedding finery, they'd plunged in among the children and dogs to be indiscriminately pawed and hugged.

"I'm thinking of that night you called and woke me, screaming that we'd won the big lottery," Star said. "And now, here we are. Who could have foreseen what a train of events that started!"

"I remember something I read someplace, 'There are people who have money and people who are rich.'"

They surveyed the sunlit meadow filled with friends, laughter, children and dogs. Darren was extracting D3 from his sling to be handed over to Jessie for a cuddle. Larry was twirling Katie and Jenny in a wild dance, the little girls' dresses flying out like colorful kites. Joy was hugging Sam around the neck and being thoroughly covered in sloppy kisses. Rowan and the boys had shed their shoes, rolled up their trousers and were wading and splashing in the stream.

Waiter and waitresses in white shirts and black aprons circulated among the guests, passing out flutes of champagne for the adults and paper cups of Kool-Aid for the children. Star raised her glass in a toast to the world:

"Here's to the richest people on Earth!"

The End

ABOUT THE AUTHOR

Doris Reidy was a bookworm before she could read. In fact, her family grew to dread the cry, "Read to me!" After her first-grade teacher gave her the gift of literacy (for which she is forever grateful), her love affair with books grew exponentially. Now, having read thousands, she's writing a few of her own and has developed a new respect for what it takes to put words on paper.

Five for the Money is her first published novel, but it won't be her last. She has others in the works, including a short story collection that's sure to find a wide audience.

Made in the USA
Charleston, SC
16 October 2016